CW00557932

LANCELOT AND THE LORD
OF THE DISTANT ISLES

LANCELOT AND THE LORD OF THE DISTANT ISLES

or, *THE BOOK OF GALEHAUT* RETOLD

by Patricia Terry and Samuel N. Rosenberg

with wood engravings by Judith Jaidinger

David R. Godine  *Publisher ✦ Boston*

First published in 2006 by
David R. Godine, Publisher
Post Office Box 450
Jaffrey, New Hampshire 03452
www.godine.com

Copyright © 2006 by
Patricia Terry and Samuel N. Rosenberg
Illustrations copyright © 2006 by Judith Jaidinger

All rights reserved. No part of this book may be used or reproduced
in any manner whatsoever without written permission, except in
the case of brief excerpts embodied in critical articles and reviews.
For information contact Permissions, David R. Godine, Publisher,
9 Hamilton Place, Boston, Massachusetts, 02108.

Library of Congress Cataloging-in-Publication Data
Terry, Patricia Ann, 1929–
[Lancelot and the Lord of the Distant Isles] Lancelot and the Lord
of the Distant Isles or, The book of Galehaut retold /
by Patricia Terry and Samuel N. Rosenberg ;
with wood engravings by Judith Jaidinger. — 1st ed.
p.   cm.
ISBN 1-56792-324-0 (alk. paper)
1. Arthurian romances—Adaptations. 2. Lancelot (Legendary
character)—Fiction. 3. Grail—Fiction. I. Rosenberg, Samuel N.
II. Jaidinger, Judith, 1941– III. Title. IV. Title: Book of Galehaut.
PS3570.E729L36   2006
813'.54—dc22
2006023168

First Edition
Printed in the United States of America

CONTENTS

INTRODUCTION

One of the greatest distinctions of the Arthurian legend is the widespread longing that it be real. If Arthur did, in fact, exist, he was probably the leader of the native people of Britain, at a time when their lands were being invaded and settled by Saxons and other Germanic groups. (These new-comers would later be called "the English.") Sometime toward the end of the fifth century, the Britons began to fight back. There was a decisive battle, and then, for perhaps half a century, the Saxons were held at bay. The memory of the chieftain responsible for that victory would have lingered long after the Saxons' ultimate success. There must have been nostalgia for a time when extraordinary valor, combined with a sense of being in the right, had prevailed over formidable, and foreign, opponents. Such was the stuff of legends carried through Wales and across the Channel into Brittany by descendants of the Celtic Britons. Even today, there are autonomy-minded Bretons in France who evoke their lost leader, "the once and future king." Chroniclers did not give him a name until the ninth century, but long before that he had come to be known as Arthur.

In the early twelfth century, when King Arthur was well established in chronicles, stories, and local traditions, Geoffrey of Monmouth wrote, in Latin, a largely imaginary *History of Britain*. From this source the most familiar aspects of Arthur's story were to be gradually elaborated, mainly in French: his birth, contrived by Merlin's sorcery; the sword Excalibur, forged in Avalon; the Round Table and the knights who had their places at it; Gawain the loyal nephew and Mordred the rebellious son; Kay the seneschal; Guenevere, Arthur's queen. To Arthur came knights from many countries, forming a company of the elite. Women, Geoffrey wrote, in a suggestion of enormous consequence, would give their hearts only to the brave.

Arthur, in Geoffrey's telling, is a great monarch. He conquers Saxons, Scots, Picts, in his own island, often with great cruelty, then makes war on Gaul, and finally attacks even Rome. His preferred city is Carleon, where he is crowned in an impressive ceremony attended by four kings. Arthur's armies are formidable, but he himself is always in the foreground, the greatest of warriors, capable of overcoming even a monstrous giant. He attracts worthy men by his reputation for valor, and is also celebrated for his generosity. When he ultimately falls in battle, it is only through the treachery of one of his own, Mordred, and it is suggested that there will be a wondrous healing of his wounds on the mythic isle of Avalon.

Geoffrey's book, however fanciful, is in the form of a chronicle, purporting to be the translation of an ancient British source. Geoffrey is rightly credited, however, with being the father of Arthurian romance, fiction derived from his work as well as other sources and no longer composed in Latin. Chrétien de Troyes, writing in French verse, developed his own version of Arthur's court as a setting for plots which reflected contemporary interest in elegance of manners, youth and beauty, ceremonial festivities, the quest for personal glory, and love. This is the modern vision of Camelot, although Chrétien almost always placed the court in Carleon.

Instead of armies in which individual exploits are subordinated to the glory of the king, Chrétien gives center-stage to the knights themselves. They leave the court in search of adventures to test their valor, and often their quest is complicated by the rival demands of love. They work out their destinies alone, sending messages back to let Arthur know their progress. While they pride themselves on being members of his court, the king himself is essentially inactive.

Thanks to the Norman Conquest in 1066, Chrétien knew France and the land beyond the Channel as a reasonably cohesive cultural entity. But King Arthur was British, the symbolic ruler of a race that prevailed before both Normans and Saxons. His knights and vassals, on the other hand, were diverse in origin, and often had lands of their own. Although some have suggested a political motivation for Arthur's diminished role in Chrétien's portrayal, that lesser role may simply reflect the need to choose between the past deeds of an already powerful monarch and the present feats of his knights. An individual, riding out on his own, ready to confront whatever challenge may come his way, is the characteristic figure of romance.

Geoffrey was Welsh and spun his tale, in part, from Celtic folk stories imbued with the magic of a pagan mythology. In his *History*, Arthur has two hundred philosophers who read his future in the stars, and a cleric who can cure any illness through prayers. Above all, Geoffrey created the prophet and magician Merlin, centrally important to the career of King Arthur. Still, he was chary in his relation of what the French would call marvels. Chrétien proves more receptive. He gives us strange fountains, mysterious maidens bearing messages, companionable lions, hints that there exists another realm independent of our own and more powerful. This inheritance from lost Celtic tales is fragmentary in Chrétien's romances, but becomes more pervasive in the expansive French narratives that dominate vernacular romance in the early decades of the thirteenth century.

Chrétien seems to have been reticent about what later came to be called "courtly love," a term invented by Gaston Paris in the nineteenth century. There is a faint trace of it in Geoffrey of Monmouth's statement connecting "the brave" and "the fair," but it was first elaborated, from yet ill-defined sources, by the lyric poets of southern France, the twelfth-century troubadours. Fundamental, and revolutionary, in this phenomenon is the belief that a man can be ennobled through striving for a woman's love. A corollary – assumed rather than logically necessary – is that love is incompatible with marriage, because true love must be free of social constraint. Erotic passion, in antiquity, was considered a disaster, a curse from the gods, and the warriors of early medieval French epic poems had essentially no interest in women, except as a form of property. It was a radical transformation when, at least in literature, a knight could be regarded as lacking prestige unless he won the love of a noble lady. He would devote himself to performing heroic deeds, but at least as much to a discreet courtship of his beloved, in the hope that she would consider him worthy of her favor. Occasionally he might even be granted a transcendent physical proof of her acceptance. From this we derive the homage that Western literature has paid to passionate, adulterous, and, almost inevitably, tragic love ever since the twelfth century.

The Arthurian romances of Chrétien de Troyes, however, do not reflect this trend, since they most often are concerned with finding a means to reconcile the demands of a knight's career with his desire for a happy marriage. The exception among his romances is a story of Lancelot called *The Knight of the Cart*, whose plot and meaning were both provided by the poet's patron, Marie de Champagne, granddaughter of Duke William IX of Aquitaine, the first known troubadour, and daughter of Eleanor of Aquitaine. It was she, presumably, who first imagined the exemplary knight in love with King Arthur's wife, Guenevere. Chrétien does not relate the beginning of Lancelot's love for the queen but concentrates on a later episode in their relationship: the queen has been abducted, and Lancelot abruptly appears, already on his way to rescue her. The abduction of the queen seems to be a Celtic motif, and the hero's name, Lancelot du Lac, may have had a Celtic source as well. Chrétien writes briefly of Lancelot's having been raised by a fairy who gave him a magic ring, capable of distinguishing enchantments from realities. The fairy will come to help him whenever he is in need.

The cart mentioned in Chrétien's title suggests the guiding principle of the story: the true lover must be ready to sacrifice even his honor for the sake of his beloved. In this first test of his devotion, Lancelot can only rescue the queen if he agrees to ride in a vehicle considered shameful because it was used for the transport of criminals. The knight hesitates, though only for a few seconds. When her freedom has been restored, the queen refuses to see him, outraged by this evidence of imperfection in his love. Later, he is given a chance to redeem himself during a tournament. Guenevere requests that he behave like a coward, and he does so, with no sign of distress.

The intensity of Lancelot's love causes him almost to lose his mind; he is so lost in adoration that he notices nothing of the world around him; he is so determined to reach his beloved that he can find the strength to wrench iron bars apart; he is so moved by finding the queen's comb, with some of her hairs caught in it, that he venerates it like a holy relic. The queen acknowledges her own passion only when she believes that Lancelot has died. The tale is filled with odd and marvelous adventures and with much that can be seen as unsympathetic caricaturing of "courtly" love. Chrétien left it to be finished by a colleague, whether from disapproval or simply loss of interest is not known. But the adulterous relationship of Lancelot and Guenevere had now found a permanent place in Arthurian legend.

INTRODUCTION

The work with which we are concerned here is an anonymous series of early thirteenth-century French prose romances collectively called the *Lancelot-Grail*, or *Arthurian Vulgate Cycle*.* It narrates in elaborate and leisurely detail the rise and fall of King Arthur, intertwining a chronicle of politics and warfare, chivalry and love with the sorcery of Merlin and the quest for the Holy Grail. It is a broadly ranging fiction, expressive of the ideals, realities and underlying questions of its time, uncomfortably caught between a Christian imperative and the vibrant memory of a pagan past. Of the five romances – *The History of the Holy Grail, The Story of Merlin, Lancelot, The Quest for the Holy Grail, The Death of King Arthur* – *Lancelot* is by far the longest and most luxuriantly filled with character and incident. The story of Lancelot and the queen is fully developed here and in the fifth romance, where it will reach its unhappy end, along with the downfall of the kingdom.

Many motifs connect *The Knight of the Cart* with the *Prose Lancelot*, among them the hero's discovery of his eventual tomb, and the extreme deference that he shows to the queen, but the spirit of the prose work is entirely different. Two factors are particularly important: magic and a new understanding of love.

The helpful fairy mentioned by Chrétien has now become

* The entire cycle, along with an early sequel, is available in English in the five volumes of *Lancelot-Grail: The Old French Arthurian Vulgate and Post-Vulgate in Translation*, Norris J. Lacy, general editor (New York and London: Garland Publishing [now Routledge], 1992–95).

the Lady of the Lake. Named Niniane, or Viviane, she has a prior history connected with that of Merlin, who attempted to seduce her. Knowing that Merlin's father was a devil, she only pretended to accept him, trading illusory favors for his knowledge of sorcery. In the end, she has learned enough to confine the magician in an invisible tomb from which he will never emerge. Among the gifts she has learned from Merlin is an ability to foretell the future.

Thus it can be assumed that when the Lady of the Lake carries off the infant Lancelot, to raise him in her magical kingdom concealed by the semblance of a lake, she does so as an agent of his fate. He grows up believing her to be his mother, and even after he has apparently been released from her influence and fallen in love with the queen, the Lady of the Lake still shapes his life. In times of danger she sends him magical weapons, she heals him when a fit of madness has brought him close to death, and she encourages Guenevere in her illicit love. She is not deterred by her foreknowledge that that love will ultimately destroy the Arthurian kingdom. On the contrary, it would seem that she has extended her hatred of Merlin to include his protégé King Arthur, born thanks to Merlin's sorcery. In our retelling of the story, the final gesture of her own magic is to slip Excalibur, which has been Arthur's sword, into Lancelot's tomb.

Lancelot lives in exile from a land he has never known, from a royal birthright he has never made an effort to recover.

His real homeland is the Lady's domain, and it seems indeed to be real in every way. But it is an otherworldly, enchanted place, and no one who meets him in later life can fail to find him correspondingly extra-ordinary. His exceptional beauty is always mentioned – and beauty, in medieval times as well as today, was regarded as a sign of a person's moral worth. There is a radiance about Lancelot as a child, and a physical ease, so that everything comes naturally to him, whether it be reading or riding fine horses or jousting. The intensity of emotion that will characterize him as an adult is shown, in his early years, by his response to perceived injustice. When the Lady, for a moment, seems somewhat remote, he is ready to gallop away in the direction of King Arthur. He does not notice that she is in distress, having realized that her cherished ward has reached the age when he must leave her and become a knight. Later on, he will not always notice the grief of others.

A certain insensitivity is useful in a hero. Lancelot, when he fights, is more a force of nature than a man. He is impersonal also in his ignorance of his past, of his lineage. The Lady, bidding him farewell at Arthur's court, reveals that she is not his mother, but tells him little more about his identity. In the white armor she had given him, he goes out alone into the world looking for trials of his prowess. The greatest of these is his conquest of Dolorous Guard, a victory not only over forces that had defeated many famous knights, but also over the supernatural. In the aftermath, he discovers not only the tomb where he will be buried but also learns his very name, and that he is the son of King Ban. The discovery is to remain his secret, however, until much later.

Perhaps this revelation seems to him merely abstract. Or perhaps he feels unworthy of such a heritage, despite his extraordinary accomplishments. The *Prose Lancelot* offers no speculations. What is clear is that when he turns once again toward King Arthur's court, the White Knight, who might be recognized, takes on a new persona as the Red Knight, whose valiant performance on the battlefield will be surpassed on a subsequent occasion by the even more impressive Black Knight. No one imagines a connection between the Lady's beautiful youth dressed in white and this warrior on whom King Arthur's very survival has come to depend.

Before Lancelot's return, King Arthur was challenged by Galehaut, Lord of the Distant Isles, a realm almost as mysterious as the domain where Lancelot had spent his childhood. Galehaut's mother, we are told, was a giantess, and we learn, from another thirteenth-century source, that his father imposed such cruel customs on visitors as to make his son prefer a life of exile. Galehaut's ambition was nothing less than conquest of the world, and so far he had known nothing but success. By the time he sent his challenge to Arthur, he had conquered twenty-eight kingdoms, whose rulers, recognizing his inherent nobility, had then become his devoted allies.

Such was Galehaut's sense of personal honor that he broke off his first engagement with King Arthur, whose forces were so weak that he seemed an unworthy opponent. That they had not been immediately overthrown was due solely to the presence of a stranger, identified only as the Red Knight. Arthur was given a truce to increase the strength of his army, but the Red Knight had disappeared. Without him, there seemed to be no hope of defeating Galehaut. When the fighting resumed, a year later, both armies were larger than before. Again an unknown knight, this time in black armor, fought for Arthur, and prevented a total rout on the first day. This time he had the assistance of Galehaut himself.

The Lord of the Distant Isles had seen countless great warriors in battle, but in Lancelot he witnessed something completely unprecedented. Men of both armies had described him as "winning the war all by himself." Now the last of Lancelot's horses had been killed under him, and he stood "like a battle flag on the field," surrounded by dead and wounded knights, yet seeming himself invincible; those who would have attacked him, alone and on foot as he was, drew back. The sight, for Galehaut, had the force of a revelation. The whole course of his life turned around at that moment; no kingdom, he thought, would be worth the death of such a knight.

Lancelot, being mortal, might well have died that day, had Galehaut not supplied him with horses and ordered his men not to attack when the knight was on foot. We do not know what Galehaut intended by inviting Lancelot to his camp after the battle, but presumably it had to do with his desire to give expression to his admiration. He might have wondered how closely the Black Knight was attached to King Arthur. We also do not know the nature of Galehaut's reaction when he discovered that the valiant helmeted warrior, once disarmed, was also a paragon of manly beauty. What is certain, however, is that he did not hesitate to grant Lancelot's wish that he surrender to Arthur; moreover, he would have done so immediately, without staging a dramatic renunciation of victory only after having proven his might in battle. But any plan desired by Lancelot was a plan that Galehaut was prepared to execute, and Lancelot wanted King Arthur not only saved from defeat but saved through his intervention. Henceforth, Arthur would owe his realm to the Black Knight. And Galehaut would have yielded all the grand ambitions of his life in exchange for having Lancelot as his companion.

To Guenevere the young knight responded as both fearless warrior and timid lover. She, however, perceived nothing of either. Seeing the disguised black-armored defender, she would scarcely have remembered the youth dressed in white whom she once dismissed with a kind but meaningless word; and later she was more amused than impressed on learning that, when Lancelot conquered Dolorous Guard, and then held back the huge armies of Galehaut, the memory of that word loomed large as his inspiration. A simple mistake! She can hardly be faulted for being what she was: a queen, experienced in the world, perhaps disenchanted, the most beautiful of women, of whom it was said she ennobled all who came into her presence. If the king had loved her once, little of that was left but ceremony, and now affairs of the heart seemed to her an inconsequential game. Thus, having accepted Lancelot's love in the tale's remarkable scene of avowal, she could assign the Lady of Malehaut to his friend, simply to make a foursome, and to have a confidante. Fear and sorrow would eventually change her, but, almost always, she would let herself be ruled by expediency.

If King Arthur could be said to do the same, it was in his instinctive refusal to perceive Lancelot as a threat to his marriage. No doubt he relied on Lancelot too much: Lancelot the greatest warrior in the world, Lancelot who made the peace with Galehaut, Lancelot who could defend his realm from endless threats of invasion. Arthur only thought to draw him closer to his court, to keep him there as a knight of the Round Table. One could say that he was credulous, or, convinced of his own greatness, could not imagine a rival for the queen's love. He himself, however, was easily and frequently seduced. He was also given to hasty, and damaging, decisions. When he had a last chance to save his kingdom, he lost it out of pride, or perhaps out of dignity. There was dignity, at least, in his final moments, and ambiguity as well. Whether the king has foreseen it or not, the hand that rises from the lake to seize his sword Excalibur will place it in Lancelot's grave, suggesting that the weapon always identified with Arthur more truly belongs to the younger warrior. Arthur himself is borne away by his half-sister Morgan. Her appearance at this point is darkly disturbing, for she has been, throughout the romance, an agent of evil, attempting to use Lancelot in order to destroy the queen. Now she takes possession of Arthur, who goes with her willingly; his mortal wounds will perhaps be healed in Avalon. Whatever we may think of this alliance, it could hardly surprise the Lady of the Lake. For her it can only be a final justification of her enmity.

The trajectory of the fictional King Arthur reproduces that of the early Britons when the chaos of Saxon invasions gave way to a time of peace and confidence, only to be reduced to chaos again, and finally defeat. When Uther Pendragon, Arthur's father, died, his son was too young to dominate the kingdom. The barons fought for the kingship, and there was no safety for anyone, anywhere. With Merlin's help, Arthur prevailed. The kingdom was powerful, its borders secure, and King Arthur's court became a source of reliable justice.

At the time of our story, this is no longer true. Lancelot provides a kind of last hope, a vision of a knight as knights were imagined to be. But he alone cannot defend the realm against an enemy as powerful as Galehaut. And Galehaut, deflected from his conquest by his love of Lancelot, then spurred by that very love to satisfy Lancelot's yearning for the queen, makes possible the adultery that will eventually destroy the court of Arthur from within.

After King Arthur, as the Lady of Malehaut says in the end to Guenevere, the kingdom is even worse off than it was when Uther died, since Arthur leaves neither son nor heir.

Excalibur lies magically in the grave with Lancelot, the grave he shares with Galehaut, and of all the participants in the drama, only one, the Lady of the Lake, remains undiminished.

℘ The story of Lancelot and Guenevere has, since the twelfth century, been part of every significant account of King Arthur. The second, overlapping, love story related in the *Prose Lancelot*, in which Galehaut, Lord of the Distant Isles, sacrificed his power, his happiness, and ultimately his life for the sake of Lancelot, has been wholly forgotten.

Lancelot is the book that Paolo and Francesca have been reading in the fifth canto of the *Inferno* when they yield to their love. Dante mentions Galehaut in passing as the intermediary between Lancelot and the queen, and Boccaccio, moved by the great lord's generosity, uses his name as the subtitle of his *Decameron* ("Il Principe Galeotto"). But in later imaginings of the Arthurian saga itself, Galehaut, for all his prominence in the original narrative, was rapidly marginalized and even eclipsed. The greatest retelling in English, the fifteenth-century work of Thomas Malory, reduced the character to one of no significance, leaving Guenevere without a rival for Lancelot's affections, and subsequent novels, plays, poems – now films as well – have accepted that simplification of the tale. Indeed, so obscure has Galehaut become that modern readers sometimes take the name to be a mere variant of Galahad – a gross mistake. Galahad is the "pure," the "chosen," knight who achieves the quest for the Holy Grail in a part of the Arthurian legend quite distinct from the story that concerns us here. There is no connection between the two figures.

What accounts for the fate of Galehaut since the Middle Ages is not at all clear, though one may certainly suspect political embarrassment: the character is, after all, King Arthur's outstanding adversary and would have defeated him easily, had he not fallen in love with Lancelot. Moral disapproval may also explain it, since the Old French text is wholly sympathetic to the homoerotic relationship. Certainly, in the case of Malory, various factors may be adduced, including the writer's general inclination to concentrate on tales of chivalry rather than love, treating love with a prudish aversion not characteristic of the French romance; and his readiness to draw from several sources – not only the *Prose Lancelot* – with a consequent de-centering of Lancelot by the inceasingly salient figure of Tristan. Moreover, Malory was surely aware of the need for caution in handling conflicts and alliances that might too readily be taken to reflect, perhaps with dangerous partiality, the troubled state of Britain in the latter half of the fifteenth century. Galehaut, powerful and ambitious, taking aim at Arthur's England from a region readily perceived as Wales, would too strongly have suggested contemporary tensions between the Crown and its Welsh adversaries for the writer not to fear charges of supporting the wrong side. Nor could Malory ignore the perils of seeing his narrative interpreted in the light of the ongoing dynastic struggles between Lancastrians and Yorkists, the so-called Wars of the Roses.

Whatever the cause of Galehaut's fading, it was obvious to us that the character deserved to be rescued from oblivion – or, for some, from the opprobrium attached, wrongly, to his action in bringing Lancelot and Guenevere together. Ours has been a work of restoration. The masses of detail and the labyrinthine complications of the original obscure, for modern readers, the great double love-story which we have tried to bring to light. To the best of our knowledge, in all the broad corpus of modern fiction derived from the Arthurian legend no such attempt has hitherto been made. Isolating the major strands of *Lancelot* and, to a lesser extent, *The Death of King Arthur*, we have rewoven them into a spare recounting for our time. Such treatment has the further advantage of making apparent the central irony of the plot: Lancelot proved indispensable to King Arthur but also became the instrument by which the Arthurian kingdom was destroyed. Without Galehaut's solicitude, the fateful adultery would not have occurred.

Like the original, our retelling concentrates on character and incident, with little concern for the explicit depiction of milieu common in modern novels. Description of persons and places remains minimal and suggestive, just as the flow of time is noted without consistent precision. In the same spirit, we have often presented dialogue bare of comment or, as happens frequently in the medieval text, in fragments emerging

directly from the narrator's prose. We have, of course, preserved the supernatural elements as integral parts of the tale
and so inherent to its universe that they appear continuous
with the natural. In our retelling, as in its source, there are thus
crucially important otherworldly beings and dwellings, enchantments and magical events, and fabulous enhancements
of reality. These may even be said to shape the story.

We have preserved, as well, characteristic modes of behavior that may be unfamiliar to modern readers, whose understanding of chivalry tends to emphasize its idealistic aspects.
When people today think of the strong protecting the weak,
or the transformation of warfare by the imposition of rules –
such as the obligation to show mercy to an opponent who
surrenders, or the equation of true nobility with generosity
and refinement of manners – they tend to forget that knights
live as warriors in a context of violence. Knights are always in
a state of readiness for battle, and scarcely know what to do in
a time of peace; thus Galehaut's men regret the imposition of
a truce, and Lancelot, on Galehaut's isolated island, complains
that they are wasting their time. In the intensity of warfare
they find their truest way of being, and it leads to a kind of
forthrightness in the expression of emotion. Warriors in epic
poems, as well as in the literature of romance, readily shed
tears, and even faint. But modern athletes, too, may have tears
in their eyes, whether at moments of victory or defeat.

Another aspect of epic poetry preserved in chivalric
romance is the theme of male companionship. Like Achilles

and Patroclus in the *Iliad*, Roland and Oliver in *The Song of Roland* know nothing of the courtly idea that a man can be ennobled by devotion to a woman. Galehaut and Lancelot would have been just like them, had it not been for Guenevere. Indeed, an important aspect of our story is its playing out of the conflict between that ancient warrior tradition and the emergence of a new, competing ethos. It should be noted in passing that, whatever else in the narrative may give evidence of homoeroticism in the relationship of Lancelot and Galehaut, the sharing of a bed does not by itself point in that direction, for such sharing, by men or by women, seems to have been common enough in the Middle Ages as an expression of friendship (or practicality) with no erotic overtones.

It may be useful to point out as well a central trait of the feudal society depicted in our book: it was a polity held together by bonds of reciprocal obligation. Lancelot's first adventure after becoming a knight offers an example. If the Lady of Nohaut calls upon King Arthur for protection, it is because he is her "liege lord." She, as his "vassal," "holds" her "fief" from him, meaning either that he gave her title to her land in return for economic and/or military service, or that she pledged such service from her estate in return for royal protection. In either case, if her own people cannot defend Nohaut against invaders, it is the king's duty to provide the defense – which here takes the form of Lancelot's engagement as her champion. It will be in essence a trial by combat, and it will be but the first in Lancelot's career.

In such confrontations, it is understood that, however un-even the contending forces may be, God will guide the right side to victory. This was an integral part of the medieval judicial system, a way of resolving disputes when an accused person had no clear proof of innocence. The practice was not infrequently used to settle even disputes concerning Church property, although it was periodically condemned by conservative clerics. A well-ordered appeal to divine judgment clearly marked an advance over undisciplined violence or the arbitrary imposition of seigniorial power. Trials presided over by a disinterested human judge and subject to the deliberations of a jury were not yet the norm at the time of our story. And the possible contradiction between an apparently God-sanctioned combat and a Christian doctrine opposed to fighting seems not to have troubled too many people. In literary works, a trial by combat frequently entails such an imbalance of contending forces that the protagonist's victory will appear inexplicable if not for the beneficent will of God. In the trial at Nohaut, Lancelot is young and inexperienced, his opponent a formidable warrior. Later on, when he fights for Guenevere, Lancelot will insist on facing three opponents at once.

⊄ Unlike our Old French source, we have stripped the legend of everything not closely related to the development of Lancelot's affective life and the role of Galehaut in that evolution. Thus, various subplots and missions involving one or another knight of the Round Table have been omitted, including some exciting magical adventures and, most notably, all traces of the quest for the Holy Grail (an episode that occurs after Galehaut's death). We have eliminated a host of characters, reduced the presence of others, and even reshaped the trajectories of a few.

All changes have been made in the interest of tightening the story without distorting the fundamentals of the original narrative. In any case, it was our intention, not to prepare either a translation or an abridgment of the Old French source, but to retell the central love-drama in such a way as to restore its complexity and emotional depth for the modern reader.

LANCELOT AND THE LORD OF THE DISTANT ISLES

PART ONE

BEFORE THE BIRTH OF KING ARTHUR, MERLIN THE SORCERER MADE THIS PROPHECY:

From the Distant Isles will come a wondrous dragon. Flying left and right over many lands, he will constantly grow in power as he subdues them. When he reaches the kingdom of Logres, his shadow will be so vast that it will darken the whole realm. The dragon will have thirty heads all made of gold. Logres will not fall, because a magnificent leopard will hold the invader back and put him at the mercy of the ruler that the dragon was on the very point of defeating. Later there will be such love between the dragon and the leopard that they will feel they are one being, each unable to live without the other. But a golden-headed serpent will steal the leopard away and corrupt his heart. And that is how the great dragon will die. ❖ Then the kingdom he spared will be lost, and the king, who had brought it forth from chaos, will leave it to chaos again. The dragon, that great lord who saved what it found most worthy in the world, at the cost of everything it most desired, will never reappear, except in stories.

BOOK ONE + THE BOY

BESIDE A LAKE SO VAST IT EXTENDED beyond the horizon, the exhausted travelers stopped for the night. Anxious as they were, sleep seemed impossible, but the sound of the water lapping against the shore gradually calmed them, while fatigue overcame the hardness of the ground. At dawn King Ban mounted his still weary horse and rode to the top of a nearby hill for one more sight of Trebe. This was the last of all his castles, and would remain to him only as long as it could hold out against the besiegers. With the queen, their infant son, and just one squire, he had followed a hidden path through the marshes that kept out invaders from the south. Trebe would be in the care of his seneschal while Ban traveled by land and sea to King Arthur's court. One after another, his allies had fallen to King Claudas; appeals to Arthur, busy with wars at home, had remained unanswered. The seneschal had urged Ban to go to Camelot himself, the better to make Arthur understand his dire need for help. Now Ban, barely on his way, could see in the distance the great walls of Trebe with the early light upon them, and the high tower. Would he succeed, he wondered, in saving this final vestige of his kingdom?

What looked like a patch of mist suddenly became a dense cloud of black in which the tower disappeared and, even as he watched, the castle was enveloped in smoke and flame. Then there was fire everywhere, making torches of lofty halls and turning the sky blood red; and all the land around reflected the hideous brightness.

King Ban knew that he had lost all hope on earth, that he would never regain his kingdom, for he was old and powerless and his son was far too young to help him. He and his lovely highborn wife would live henceforth in exile, dependent on charity, condemned to poverty and sorrow, although he had been a mighty king. In the shock of this understanding, he fell unconscious from his horse, hitting his head so hard that the blood rushed from his ears and nose. He lay senseless on the ground. After a time, he half-opened his eyes, conscious enough to ask God's forgiveness for his sins, "and I beg you, Lord, to watch over my wife, Elaine, who, by her lineage, belongs to the House of David, but who now lacks all protection in the world. I commend to you the life of my infant son, knowing that the most defenseless orphan has a true father in you, and no one is so weak that you cannot give him power." With his last strength he plucked three blades of grass, a sign of the Holy Trinity.

King Ban's stallion, frightened by his master's fall, had galloped down to the lake, where the other horses were standing. Alarmed, the queen called to the squire, who caught the stallion and rode in the growing light to the top of the hill. He found the king lying dead. The queen heard the young man's loud cry, put the baby down, and, holding up her skirts, ran through the thick brush to where the squire was weeping beside his lord's body. She fainted at the sight, regaining her senses only to fill the air with lamentation for her valiant husband, the noble king, now lost to her forever in this life. She was pleading with God to let her die with him, when the thought of her baby suddenly broke in on her grief. She could almost see the helpless child under the hooves of the horses! Half mad with terror, she began running back down the hill, crying for help, stumbling, overwhelmed by the thought that he might have been trampled. Branches tore at her hair, drew blood from her face. By the time she reached the shore of the lake, it was broad daylight. The queen saw her baby, untouched by the horses, lying naked in the lap of a young woman who was smiling at him, caressing him, lifting him up to hold him tight against her breast, kissing his eyes and mouth, and no wonder! for the beauty of the child was truly astonishing.

Queen Elaine cried, "My child! Please, dear sweet lady, for God's sake, give me the child! He'll have suffering enough, for his father has just died, and now he is alone in the world, robbed of the many lands which should have been his." The stranger made no reply, seemed not even to have heard. But when the queen drew closer, she stood up, still holding the child, and went quickly to the water's edge. Then, without so much as a glance at the queen, she put her feet together and jumped in.

Elaine would have followed her, had the squire not arrived in time to hold her back. The infant and the unknown woman had disappeared, leaving not even a ripple on the surface of the lake. The queen had lost all she loved in the world, and her grief was beyond telling. Husband and king now dead, her only child drowned or abducted to some spellbound watery depth, her past and her future were both stripped away.

On the road by the shore, an abbess was passing by with a few nuns and her chaplain. At the sound of Elaine's piteous laments, she stopped to see if she could be of help. "May God grant you comfort," she said.

"Indeed, good mother, there is no one who needs it more than I do."

The abbess saw how beautiful she was, despite her grief, and said, "Tell me who you are."

"I am a woman who has lived too long."

But the chaplain told the abbess that she was a queen, the wife of King Ban.

"No, I am only the queen of sorrows," said Elaine. "If you really wish to help me, I beg you to make me a nun. There is nothing in the world I care about now, and the world can do without me easily enough. Otherwise, I will wander in the forest until I die."

"My lady, if it is truly your desire to be a nun, we thank God that so worthy a queen will join our company. You shall have the place of honor among us, as is fitting, since your husband's forebears established and built our abbey. But please tell us what has happened to you."

The queen related how her lord had lost his kingdom, how

they had left Trebe in a desperate effort to seek King Arthur's help, how he had met his end there on the hill, and how a demon disguised as a woman had stolen her son away, "leaving me bereft of all I loved."

When her long golden hair had been shorn, she took the veil. The squire, moved by the event, renounced the world as his lady had done, there on the shore of the lake. The king's body was carried to the abbey and buried with solemn ceremony. Every day after mass, the queen would go to the lake where her son had disappeared, to remember him, to weep for her loss, and to pray.

℘ Lancelot was too young to remember anything of his life before he was carried off by the Lady of the Lake, an enchantress named Viviane who had learned her arts from Merlin. The great wizard had lost both heart and judgment to her great beauty, and Viviane had used all her wiles to delude him, knowing that his father was a devil who had seduced a mortal woman. She also knew by what magical and illicit impersonation he had brought about the birth of King Arthur. In exchange for promises of love, she had persuaded him to teach her sorcery and had soon learned what she needed to imprison him, alive but sleeping, in a secret cave in a forest. Merlin was never seen again.

Lancelot grew up in the kingdom Viviane had established beneath what appeared to be an ordinary lake. In that magical place, she had fine houses, great forests full of game, even rivers and brooks. Many knights and noble ladies lived there with her. Only the mother who had borne him could have loved Lancelot more than the Lady of the Lake. Never did he imagine he was not her son. She gave him the most tender care, finding a lovely young woman to nurse him and, after he was weaned, an understanding tutor, suitable for a young boy. When he was three years old, he looked as if he were five. No one had ever seen a more beautiful child, and his beauty only increased as he grew older.

The Lady alone was aware of Lancelot's true identity. While the people of her household referred to him as "the child," the Lady liked to call him "my prince," and would tell him how hard it was to be worthy of a crown, but she seemed to be only teasing. When he asked about his father, she would only say he had been a very great man. He imagined someone taller and stronger than anyone around him, some warrior even more valiant than the heroes of whom poets sang, a man to whom he could give his admiration and his love.

The Lady taught him all that makes a noble life, and provided him with companions of his own age, including, after a while, his cousins Lionel and Bors. He learned to ride fine horses and to hunt. In little time, he acquired the rudiments of jousting and soon surpassed his mentors. He liked playing checkers and chess, and read with pleasure. He sang wonderfully well, though he did so rarely. In form he was both graceful and powerful, everything about him perfectly proportioned, although his chest was unusually large. In later years, Queen Guenevere would say that God had made him so to accommodate the great size of his heart.

Even as a young child he had exquisite manners, delighted more in giving than in receiving, and was kind and gentle to everyone. But injustice of any kind aroused in him such fury that his bright and joyful eyes turned black as coals, his cheeks became blood red, his voice rang out like a trumpet, and it was difficult to calm him down. He believed that he was strong enough to accomplish whatever it was in his heart to do.

❡ One day, when Lancelot was eighteen, he went hunting in the forest, where he never failed to bring down some worthy prey. This time, however, his quarry was exceptional – a stag of immense size, which he killed with a single arrow. He sent it as a gift to the Lady. He himself rested for a while through the heat of the afternoon, and then rode home. The Lady saw him arrive, sitting his horse with the grace of a born rider. He was dressed all in green, with a garland on his head, like springtime itself, she thought, or the promise of fruit not yet ripe, and her eyes filled with tears. When the youth came to greet her, she turned aside, weeping. He asked what was wrong, but she didn't reply. At last she uttered a few words, ordering him to go away. Confused and upset, he rushed back to the courtyard where he had left his horse. He had just mounted again when she reappeared, seized the bridle, and told him to dismount. When they were alone in her room, she asked where he had intended to go.

"Since you were angry with me, and wouldn't tell me why, I thought I would go to King Arthur and ask to be made a knight."

She laughed at him, saying that he had no idea how courageous a knight had to be, how ready to risk his life for anyone who might need his help. What made him think, she asked, that he was capable of valor? "Your valor has never been tested." In truth, she knew very well that he was by nature proof against fear and would freely sacrifice a life of comfort for the opportunity of winning the highest rewards of honor, but she still had to ask the question. Though heartsick at the thought of giving him up, the Lady realized that it was time. She embraced him, weeping with regret, and promised she would take him to King Arthur. She told him this about knighthood: "In the sight of God, all human beings are equal. There came a time, however, many years ago, when the strong began to take advantage of the weak; then other men, skilled in warfare and empowered by a sense of justice, became the defenders of those unable to defend themselves. Thus there arose an order of Knighthood. Knights live in the service of all who need protection, especially widows and orphans, and the Holy Church, which relies on them as a mother relies on her sons. To be a true knight is not a privilege of birth. It is granted only to the great of heart, and to those whose deeds demonstrate their worth. A knight's true identity comes from the life he lives. A knight must achieve for himself an illustrious name. And so it will be with you."

℃ The journey that King Ban had undertaken was completed now by his son, although Lancelot had never heard his own name or his father's. That spring, not long after Whitsuntide, the Lady of the Lake, her hopeful ward, and a great retinue set out on the lengthy journey to the coast of Gaul. From there, they went by boat to Great Britain and then started on the road to King Arthur's court. It was a magnificent procession that rode across fields and through the forest toward Camelot, the horses and their riders all in white, silver, and ivory, silk and brocade. A squire carried a fine silver helmet, another a pure white shield, another a spear, another a ceremonial robe for Lancelot to wear when he was knighted. Then came the Lady in white samite, her cloak lined with ermine, riding an exquisite snow-white mare that moved as softly as a cloud. The boy who rode beside her on a tall and spirited hunter could not have been more wonderful to behold, princely in his bearing, with innocence and energy shining from his whole being. They were attended by Bors and Lionel, his young cousins, who would perhaps return this way themselves one day. No eyes could look elsewhere when the procession at last crossed the bridge into King Arthur's high city.

The king was quick to agree that so promising a youth

should become a knight. The Lady, however, insisted that he must be knighted in his own arms and attire. To this the king objected. He was accustomed to making his knights a gift of their armor, so that they would be known to belong to his household. When the Lady would not yield, Sir Yvain and Sir Gawain, both knights of the Round Table, convinced the king that an exception should be made.

So the Lady of the Lake succeeded in her mission. As she was taking leave of Lancelot, she told him for the first time that she was not his mother, although she loved him fully as much as if she were. His father was one of the noblest knights in the world, she said, and his mother one of the loveliest and most worthy ladies who ever lived. More than that, she told him, he would learn before long, but not from her. She commended him to God and kissed him and, just before leaving, said, "My prince, you will find that the more great and perilous deeds you undertake, the more you will be ready to do others. Should there be any that prove beyond your powers, be assured that no other knight on earth could accomplish them, either. So go your way with confidence, my beautiful, noble child. Your quality is such that men will always aspire to win your friendship, and women will love you above all others." Too choked with sorrow to say anything more, she embraced him once again and turned away. The boy was deeply moved, and his eyes filled with tears. Wordlessly, he kissed his cousins to bid them farewell.

THE BOY

℄ Queen Guenevere heard that the young man dressed in dazzling white who had come to court with the Lady of the Lake would be made a knight the very next morning. It was the Feast of Saint John, which some people still called Midsummer Eve. Such haste surprised her, but when the king and the two greatest knights of the realm assured her that the candidate was worthy of such an honor, she was eager to see him. Sir Gawain had promptly taken charge of the stranger, inviting him to rest and refresh himself in the comfort of his lodgings. In this welcome the young man found a reassuring promise of friendship, a kindness never to be forgotten. Radiant with expectation, he rode with Gawain through streets thronged with the curious, all of them gazing at the youth in admiration. The king received him in the great hall. The queen was at his side, and it was the queen alone whom the newcomer saw on entering. He could scarcely believe there was such beauty in the world – even the Lady of the Lake could not be compared with her. And in this he was right, for the queen was beauty itself, and her goodness was held to be even more perfect than her beauty. It was said of her that she ennobled all who came into her presence.

When she took his hand, he jumped at her touch as if she had awakened him from sleep. She asked his name and where he came from, but he was too abashed to utter a word. The ten years of age separating them made her too remote, too intimidating. When she asked him again, very gently, he murmured that he did not know. Realizing that she herself must be the cause of his embarrassment, and not wanting to add to his discomfort, the queen said nothing further. After a while she rose and went to her rooms.

℃ That night the young man kept vigil in the church of Saint Stephen, wondering how his life would now be changed and praying for guidance. Yet always foremost in his mind was his memory of the queen. The next morning, in full armor, he knelt before the king, who touched his shoulders with the sword Excalibur. It was a jeweled and gleaming weapon, a marvel forged, it was said, by hands that were more than human, extracted by the sorcerer Merlin from an enchanted lake and entrusted to King Arthur for the duration of his life. With this sword, the king granted the young man knighthood. He gave him no sword of his own, planning to complete the ceremony later. Truth to tell, Arthur saw in this radiant youth the promise of a new and glowing presence at his Round Table. The manner of his arrival, his tie to the Lady of the Lake, his extraordinary beauty – everything suggested an exceptional destiny. The king wished to devise some special rite to mark his passage into knighthood.

The interruption pleased the youth, for he secretly hoped that the sword of knighthood would come to him from someone else. He went to take leave of the queen. Kneeling in front of her, he said, "My lady, if it please you, wherever I go in the world, and whatever I may do, it shall be as your knight."

"Thank you," she said, "that would please me very much."

"With your permission, I will leave tomorrow morning."

"Farewell, then, and God protect you, dear friend."

And he answered silently, "My lady, I thank you with all my heart for granting me that name."

BOOK TWO ✦ THE WHITE KNIGHT

THE NEW KNIGHT WAS TOO IMPATIENT to tarry at court. He longed to experience the reality of a knight's high mission, to prove his mettle and gain well-justified renown. Now with Queen Guenevere's words resounding in his heart, he felt spurred to action, and nothing could deter him from seizing the first opportunity to face a challenge. It arose that very evening, when a man, in full armor except for his helmet, strode into the great hall and stood before the king. "I serve the Lady of Nohaut," he said, "and have come, at her command, to declare, my lord, that she is in need of your help. The King of Northumberland has invaded her lands and laid siege to one of her castles, killing many of her men and destroying the land on all sides. He insists that he has done this by right, and is calling on her to keep an agreement that my lady does not acknowledge in the slightest. He insists that she yield to him unless she can find a champion to defend her – a knight willing to face two opponents simultaneously. As you are her liege lord, she asks that you send her such a knight."

Before King Arthur could say a word, the young man sprang forward to offer his help.

"My friend," said King Arthur, "this is too grave a challenge for one as inexperienced as you. You have come to me with greatness in your heart and with a yearning to win honor and fame. But it would be wrong of me to let you face such danger so soon, and it would grieve me to see all that is fresh and beautiful in you brought to an early end. We have not yet even taken the final step in making you a knight."

But the young man's persistence defeated the king's paternal reluctance to risk his safety. So Arthur agreed, and the youth rode off at once toward Nohaut and the allure of worthy combat.

Two against one: a formidable risk for any man but especially for a novice. The training he had received as an adolescent, his daring – above all, the energizing sense of being in the right – ensured his victory. In twenty minutes that left the Lady of Nohaut more breathless than her champion, the conflict was resolved in her favor; and King Arthur, had he been present, would happily have forsworn his doubts.

The battle at Nohaut was but the first trial for the new knight, resplendent in his white armor, as he wandered through the countryside, drawing appeals from the helpless and defiance from the wicked. He threw himself into these adventures with the eagerness of the young and high-minded, the thought that he was the queen's "dear friend" unleashing all the generosity of spirit fostered in him by the Lady of the Lake. He was strong and skilled. Though he suffered wounds and momentary reverses, he emerged the victor from every encounter. He freed a knight and two maidens whom he then sent with a message to the queen. He battled an ugly knight for access to a ford that the miscreant had no right to bar. He rescued a girl taunted by a giant.

℃ One day, when the White Knight was riding through a forest, he met a young woman grieving for the death of her lover, killed, like so many other knights, attempting the Adventure of Dolorous Guard, which "only the greatest knight in the world can achieve."

"What Adventure is that?"

"If you go there, you'll find out," she sadly advised him.

The young knight took the path she showed him, and galloped until he saw a superb fortress high on a cliff, with the Humber River flowing at its base. He met a woman at the gate whom he would have recognized, had her face not been heavily veiled. She told him about the castle, a dwelling place of evil, whose people were under the sway of a "wicked and powerful lord, in thrall to enchantments that embitter their lives and make them long for deliverance." The occasional knights who tried to rescue them were all they ever saw of the outside world. These were made to fight against impossible odds, and were then buried in a vast underground chamber. Strange and terrifying noises came from there; they were thought to be the voices of the unquiet dead. The castle-dwellers never saw the sun. Only gnarled, leafless trees and seedless plants grew in gardens that had once flourished. The evil lord and his vassals felt no deprivation, but those who served them toiled through the seasons wan and hungry.

The castle was surrounded by two walls, each with one small door. If a knight tried to enter, he was forced to confront ten opponents. By the rules of that combat, they fought him one at a time, but each knight could change places with another as soon as he was tired.

The lady turned away, and the knight heard someone calling from high above, "Sir knight, what do you want?"

"I want to come in."

"That will cost you dear."

"Whatever it costs, my friend, but hurry! It's getting dark."

The man on watch blew a horn, and an armed knight rode out through the narrow gate, and said, "Sir knight, we'll have more room to fight over there near the tower."

It was a quick encounter. The White Knight shattered the defender's lance and sent his own through the other's hauberk and deep into his chest. The man fell backwards off his horse, and was dead before he landed. The victor, however, had scarcely time to recover his lance when the horn sounded again and another opponent appeared. This one and three others barely survived the combat. The White Knight would have gone on fighting in the dark, had not the rest of his opponents withdrawn behind the portcullis. The young woman returned and took him to an inn in the town outside the castle walls. She let him go alone into his room. There he found three silver shields hanging on the wall, one traversed by a single red band, one with two bands on it, and one with three. This seemed to him strange and even troubling, but before he could give it any further thought, his guide came in, her face now unveiled. In the joy of recognition, he threw his arms around her, exclaiming, "Celise! You've come from my dear Lady! No messenger could be more welcome!"

The Lady of the Lake had sent Celise to bring the shields and to carry a prophetic message: the next day her prince would be master of the castle. There he would learn his father's name and his own. As for the silver shields, the first would give him twice his usual strength, the second would triple it, and the third would make him four times as strong. On no account was he to rely on the energy of youth, but must instead take up one of the shields as soon as he was tired.

℘ The next morning, the White Knight heard mass and prepared for battle. He was annoyed to discover that the five knights he had defeated the day before would count for nothing: he would have to fight ten more at the first wall, then ten at the second. The Lady's emissary, however, promised not only that he would defeat them all, but that he would never be killed while he was wearing armor. "In that case," he said, "I need not fear dying in shame."

At the castle a knight confided to him, "The truth is I wish you had taken the castle already, and put an end to my lord's cruel ways. But still I have to honor the fealty I swore."

In the jousts that followed, the White Knight taunted his opponents to make them attack two or three at a time, so impatient was he to have done with them. But as soon as one of the defenders had had enough, he withdrew into the castle, sending another to take his place. The White Knight was offered no such respite. He was out of breath and bruised and bleeding; almost nothing was left of his shield. Then a squire brought him another with one red band across it, and he immediately felt twice as strong as before, agile, swift-moving, free of pain. He fought on through the day, becoming disheartened at how long it was taking to reach his goal. The squire brought him the two-banded shield, and with its help he killed or grievously wounded all his foes except for three, who made haste to declare themselves his prisoners. But beyond the first gate there waited ten more knights. Then Celise herself brought him the third shield and a beautiful new helmet, since his own had taken so many blows it offered no protection. The White Knight objected that she was helping him too much, but she said she wanted the second gate to be even more brilliantly won than the first.

And so it was. He attacked with such ferocity that the defenders wanted only to flee as fast as they could, and the lord of the castle, Brandis, watching from the battlements, felt his confidence drain away. Should the White Knight defeat all his men, Brandis would be obliged to fight him too. He paled when the second gate was flung open and the courtyard filled with people rejoicing at his imminent loss. The crowd assured the White Knight that all he had left to do was defeat the Lord of Dolorous Guard, and the knight asked nothing better. But just as Brandis was expected to emerge, word came that the coward had instead fled in despair. The White Knight had won!

23

℃ Celise led the White Knight to a graveyard outside the walls. Tombstones displayed the names of many of King Arthur's knights, for there they were destined to lie. Among the stones the young man saw a great slab on which was written in gold that only the conqueror of Dolorous Guard would have the strength to lift it and that he would find his name inscribed underneath. Neither men nor machines had succeeded in raising this tombstone, to the great frustration of Brandis, who had always wanted to put to death the one whose name was written there. The White Knight stood imagining the weight of the slab. Then he took one end in both hands and lifted it with ease. On the under surface he read:

HERE WILL LIE
LANCELOT OF THE LAKE,
THE SON OF KING BAN OF BENOIC

At that moment it seemed he had always known. He had always felt, deep within, that "my prince" was not just an expression of motherly tenderness and that his drive for knightly prowess was a sign of heroic forebears.

He let the tombstone drop back into place before the young woman could see the inscription. Lancelot understood that, although he was a king's son, he was so in name alone. He could take no pride in his birth until he had fulfilled the promise of his parentage: only then would he identify himself.

⁋ The chambers to which the victorious White Knight was led were those that had been occupied by Brandis. They were a small part of the fortress but splendid with all the things that belonged in the court of a powerful, highborn man. Attendants disarmed their new lord and did everything they could for his pleasure and comfort. His wounds were carefully tended, and he was content to rest for a little while. This was his new home, the site that bound him to a father, the fortress that the Lady of the Lake had willed him to possess.

One day, as the White Knight was inspecting the fortifications, an old servant approached him hesitantly. She had clearly been weeping and, when the knight asked her why, urging her to confide in him, she said, "You did the great deeds required of you – deeds no knight before you had ever accomplished – but if only you could have killed Brandis!" He ruled them still, she said. When they rejoiced at the White Knight's victory, they had believed it would undo the magic spells that had made them live in the shadows, terrified and without hope. Now they realized that nothing had changed, yet no one wanted to further endanger the man who had fought so splendidly.

"What must I do?" said the new lord of Dolorous Guard.

"Evil has given Brandis terrible powers, but he is mortal. Knowing that you could defeat him in combat, he would not face you. You could search the world for him and never find him. But your courage is so great that perhaps you can destroy his creation, the cause of our misery. I am speaking of forces so great that the terror of them invades our sleep, and all our waking hours are filled with dread."

Lancelot did not hesitate. "Show me the way, good woman," he said.

℧ The servant led him down from the parapet, then, torch in hand, into a dank passageway through the rock foundation of the castle. They arrived at a wide and heavy iron door, before which the woman hesitated. Lancelot moved ahead to push it open. No sooner had he advanced across the threshold than the door swung shut behind him, leaving the old servant on the other side.

The knight was at the entrance to a vast underground room. The only light came from a small barred window quite far away, toward which the knight advanced, sword in hand. As he drew closer, there was a trembling in the ground beneath his feet, and, with the sound of huge stones splitting apart, the whole chamber began to whirl around. Clinging to the wall and crawling, he slowly made his way toward the faint glow. Suddenly, the bars fell away and the tall, narrow panel in which they had been set sprang open. Just inside the gallery now revealed, the White Knight saw two gigantic bronze figures wielding immense swords that crisscrossed in a dazzling blur across the narrow entryway. Without an instant's hesitation, he hurled himself toward them, holding his shield over his head. They struck through it so hard that the links of his hauberk split, and blood streamed from his left shoulder. He fell onto his hands, but the bronze figures were now behind him, and he went on.

Soon his way was barred by a huge well, more than seven feet across, whose water had the stench of rotting things. On the other side stood an immensely tall man whose eyes glowed like coals in his shadowy face, and from whose mouth shot bright-green flames. The giant raised an axe above his head. The knight moved back far enough to get a running start, leapt over the well and caught the blow of the axe on his shield. He would have fallen into the water, had he not seized his opponent by the throat, holding him so tightly that the giant lost his footing. The White Knight turned him toward the edge of the well and threw him in.

A beautiful bronze statue of a woman now stood where the giant had been, holding two keys in her hands. An inscription on a column in the middle of the room read:

THE LARGE KEY
OPENS THIS PILLAR.
THE SMALL KEY
WILL UNLOCK
THE PERILOUS CASKET.

He inserted the large key. Inside the column was the casket, from which came the anguished cries of people in torment; the whole chamber resonated with the sound. The knight crossed himself and, as he put the small key into the lock, a

whirlwind erupted with terrifying force and a noise so over-whelming that he fell unconscious. When he revived, he stood up painfully, took the keys and started back. Where the well had been was only the stone floor; the three bronze figures had disappeared.

He made his way outside to where the people of the castle were all waiting. Their joy on seeing him was immeasurable. He went to place the keys on the altar of the chapel and then proceeded to the great hall.

The seneschal, stepping forward from the crowd, said, "There are no words to thank you, my lord. You have brought all our misfortunes to an end. The fortress is truly yours, and you are our undisputed lord."

"Then the name of this fortress shall be changed," the White Knight declared. "Henceforth it shall be known as Joyous Guard."

The next morning there was sunlight everywhere. Gardens and orchards in bloom surrounded the castle, whose inhabitants felt that they, too, had been reborn. The days that followed were one splendid celebration.

℄ It was not long, however, before the lord of Joyous Guard was called away, having learned that Sir Gawain and nine other knights had been trapped by foes and imprisoned. When the news of Dolorous Guard had reached Camelot, these knights set out to learn if the fortress had really been taken. On their way they met a nobleman who told them that the White Knight had been killed. Their grief was immense, for they knew that this must be the young man who had come to Arthur's court with the Lady of the Lake. The nobleman, who was in truth none other than Brandis, bent on revenge, invited them to stay the night at a nearby castle. Once they were inside, a large group of armed men fell upon them. They had been prisoners ever since.

The White Knight set out to rescue them. And he did. Alone he routed the castle's well-armed force of more than a hundred men. By the time they realized that he was charging straight into them regardless of their number, he had killed so many that their companions simply fled. No one had seen so bold and forceful a warrior before. He had grown and changed since the Lady of the Lake had first sought to make him a knight, but, when the prisoners were released, Gawain knew to whom they owed their freedom. It was the very same youth, dressed all in white, whom he had once welcomed to King Arthur's court. He fell to his knees before the White Knight, trying to thank him, but the knight would not allow it: "I have never forgotten your kindness to me, my lord."

"Will you come with me now and let the court rejoice to see you again?"

"Not now, my lord. I must go and put things in order in my domain," he answered. "Please give the king and queen my respectful greetings." He bade them all farewell and rode away.

❡ Now that Gawain and his companions were at court once again, all Camelot was festive. Word had come of the White Knight's victory in the cruel combat where so many brave knights had met their end. No one could talk of anything else. But the conqueror of Dolorous Guard had yet to appear. As they dined in the great hall one evening, a man of stately mien wearing chain-mail, although his head and hands were bare, came to stand before the king but did not bow. "King Arthur, I have been sent here by the most valiant man of his generation, Galehaut, son of the Giantess and Lord of the Distant Isles. He has vanquished thirty kings, but he intends to be crowned only after he has defeated one hundred fifty kings and has possession of England – the land of Logres, as you call it. When you hold it in fief from him, he will honor you as the greatest of his vassals."

"Sir," said the king, "I have had no overlord except God, and I will not accept one now."

"Then you must lose your honor and your lands."

"God willing, I shall not."

"In that case, King Arthur, my lord formally challenges you, and will be in your domain within the month. Nor will he leave again before he has taken from you all that you possess, including your peerless queen."

"Lord knight," replied the king, "I think that I need not be unduly worried. Let both sides do their best, and we shall see what happens."

As the knight was leaving, he turned back at the door, looked straight toward the king, and said, "I grieve for you!" Then he rode away with his company of knights.

King Arthur asked his nephew, Gawain, if he had ever seen this Galehaut. He had not, and neither had several other knights who were there. But Galegantis of Wales, who had traveled widely, came forward and said, "My lord, I have indeed seen Galehaut, and he stands taller than any knight in the world. Everyone who has met him says that no one could be nobler, more gracious or more generous than he, nor has anyone of his age been so triumphant in war. He has the love of all his people. The very kings he has vanquished are now his staunchest allies. I am not saying, of course, that he is likely to defeat you. God forbid that that should happen! I would rather die instead. But Galehaut is indeed a great and formidable foe."

℧ The king went out hunting the next day after mass, and nothing more was said about Galehaut. Not long afterward, however, a message came from a lady whose fief stood on the border of the kingdom. Her lands had been invaded by the son of the Giantess and all her castles lost except two. If the king did not come soon, these also would be taken. "I'll go at once!" said the king. "How large is his army?"

"Five thousand men."

"Tell your lady that I will leave here tonight or tomorrow morning."

His men advised him to wait until he could summon more

knights, but he said, "I will never stand by idly when one of my vassals is attacked!" So with only seven hundred he set out, having sent messengers to all who owed him service. To reach their destination would take several days of hard riding.

Galehaut heard that King Arthur was arriving with only a small army. His own, apart from the horsemen, had many foot soldiers, well armed and equipped with iron-tipped arrows. They had surrounded themselves with iron nets, and thus could not be attacked from the rear. Galehaut assembled his forces and said that, since King Arthur had so few men with him, there was little need to send a vast army to meet him. Malaguin, the King of the Hundred Knights, asked for the privilege of leading the first attack. But when he looked at Arthur's forces from the top of a hill, it seemed to him that there were more than seven hundred. Preferring to err on the side of caution, he told Galehaut they had one thousand. "Then choose one thousand of your own, and go to meet him."

When it was apparent that Galehaut himself would not join the fighting, Arthur could not do so either. He sent Sir Gawain in his place, asking him to order his forces with great care, because Galehaut had the advantage in numbers. Gawain led his knights across a ford in the river near their camp, and sent his first battalion to engage the enemy. But these came on so fast that all one thousand were soon in the field. Realizing that great prowess had to compensate for weak numbers, King Arthur's men fought well, and Gawain the best of all, so that the few managed to drive back the many. The King of the

Hundred Knights sent a message to Galehaut, and three thousand reinforcements promptly arrived. Those fleeing the field turned back toward their opponents, who were dismayed to see the huge army approaching. "Now," said Gawain to his knights, "we will see who truly cares for King Arthur's honor!"

But no matter how valiantly they fought, they were forced to retreat toward the river. Thanks to Gawain's heroic efforts, many were able to cross the ford and find safety in the castle. Had it not been for him, no one would have escaped! He himself, although badly wounded, continued fighting until it was nearly dark, but then the blows and anguish of the day took their toll. Gawain fell off his horse in a faint and had to be carried to his quarters. A squire ran to inform the royal couple, who hastened to the bedside of the wounded man. They needed no doctor to describe what they could plainly see. The extent of Gawain's injuries made the king tremble lest his nephew not survive; the queen grasped her husband's hand in alarm. Neither could imagine the realm bereft of its greatest defender. Yet the fighting would resume the next day without him.

NOT FAR FROM THE BATTLEFIELD
was the town of Malehaut, ruled by a widowed
chatelaine who took her responsibilities so to
heart that her people were as one in their love
and respect for her. She cared for the poor and rewarded the
charitable; she tended the sick and offered hospitality to the
stranger. It was at her castle that Lancelot found himself at
the time of the clash between King Arthur's meager forces and
the larger numbers fighting for the Lord of the Distant Isles.

Once assured of his untroubled hold on Joyous Guard,
Lancelot had begun to feel that he had nothing further to do
there. His men would turn back anyone so foolish as to challenge their new lord. Dolorous Guard no longer existed to
offer passing knights an unprecedented adventure, and anyone who attempted to conquer Joyous Guard would find it
more than adequately defended. From Brandis's former seneschal to the youngest of the household knights, all his people
were profoundly grateful to the White Knight and ready to
demonstrate their devotion. The simple castle-dwellers themselves would not hesitate to give their lives for him.

What Lancelot felt to be his mission meant that once a
problem had been solved, he had to move on. Now he had
a home to which he could always return, and he would, of
course, think of Joyous Guard with pride and affection. But

his truest, unspoken, allegiance was to the queen; and for her he was prepared to wander through the world, seeking deeds that would bring him glory in her honor. He had placed Joyous Guard in the hands of his seneschal and set out one day in search of new adventures. He was alone, having determinedly rejected the assistance of a squire.

He had ridden for weeks, ambling alongside streams, galloping across pasturelands, toiling up wooded hills – all without any encounter that might serve his purpose. He found no victims of injustice, no fiercely armed foe, above all no hint of an enchantment; there seemed to be nothing to test his prowess. Late one afternoon, with some discouragement and with the dulled attention that fatigue can bring, Lancelot had entered a pine forest. It was growing dark, but the path seemed clear enough. Thinking he saw a light in the distance – perhaps a house where he could find shelter – he urged his horse to a gallop. That rash move came to a brutal halt! A rope had been strung between two trees. His horse pitched forward, and the last thing Lancelot heard was a sound of mocking laughter, as he landed on a heap of stones, senseless.

It was only shortly after daybreak that a team of foresters happened upon the White Knight's battered but sleeping body. They woke him gently and did their best to answer his questions. Thieves had been abroad of late, trapping the unwary and carrying off their goods. Lancelot was fortunate: he was still alive and still had his armor, though his shield and arms, like his horse, were gone. The foresters explained that the forest was part of the lands held by the Lady of Malehaut, who would surely receive the injured knight and provide well for his care. Lancelot, in pain, murmured his thanks, and the good men carried him cautiously to the lady's castle.

The chatelaine was rightly appreciated for her readiness to help. After a quick, wordless examination of the wounded stranger, she gladly accepted him as both patient and guest. It was plain that the knight was a young man of some consequence, even if he was unusually hesitant to speak of anything but gratitude. Although his face had been bruised, he was extraordinarily handsome, a fact that the still-youthful widow did not fail to notice.

ℭ The short time he was in her care sufficed for him, whether he desired it or not, to occupy a significant place in her heart. As the knight's condition improved, conversation became easier, without, however, revealing anything of his background. Blaye, the Lady of Malehaut, had not been able to learn his name, although she tried very hard to do so. She could find no way of countering the young man's adamant refusal to identify himself, and eventually realized she would need to seek the information elsewhere.

When Lancelot heard news of the battle, which was on the lips of everyone in Malehaut, he appealed to Blaye to judge him sufficiently recovered to join the fighting. He assured her that he would return to her care at night, if he was physically able to do so. She agreed, and, the next morning, gave him a horse and a red shield; he wore his own armor, now cleaned and burnished, with breaks repaired and dents smoothed out.

❡ That day, as King Arthur's battalions crossed the river, one after the other, Galehaut's men rushed to meet them, and the sharp points of spears took many a life. There was good fighting on both sides, but King Arthur's men showed greater valor, in part because they were out-numbered two to one, but more especially because they were inspired by the extraordinary prowess of a knight they could identify only by his red shield. He fought with exemplary vigor and daring, as if driven to prove himself at any cost. When darkness brought the battle to an end, they looked for that knight, knowing that he alone had stood between them and defeat, but he was nowhere to be found.

❡ Despite the day's success, Arthur began to fear that he would lose to Galehaut. He had recently experienced strange, disquieting dreams in which the hair of his head and beard dropped out or his fingers fell off. This predicted, according to the wise men whom he had quickly consulted, that his power would soon fail and his glorious kingdom not last much longer. They said he was losing the love of his people because he was ungenerous and uncaring. They accused him of failing in his duty to God, and failing also in his obligations to his allies, as witness the death of King Ban. After all, had Ban not repeatedly sought his help, only to be rebuffed by Arthur's silence? No good could come of such disloyalty. It was not surprising, then, that Arthur felt keenly threatened in his conflict with Galehaut.

℘ The next morning, Galehaut told his assembled army that he considered it dishonorable to fight against such weak forces. He sent his cousin Malaguin, the King of the Hundred Knights, and Cleolas, the First Defeated King, to Arthur, who received them with great honor. "My lord," said the King of the Hundred Knights, "we are liege men of Galehaut, Lord of the Distant Isles. He has sent us to say he had not expected that the most powerful king in the world would come here with so inadequate an army. Since fighting you in these circumstances would not enhance his honor, he offers you a truce. You shall have a whole year to prepare, at the end of which time Galehaut will nevertheless take your kingdom. And he will do so with the help of that Red Knight of yours who won the day."

King Arthur accepted this offer with what dignity he could, expressing confidence in his own eventual victory, but in his heart he was more troubled than before, particularly by Galehaut's threat that he would have the Red Knight on his side.

He went to stay at Carduel in Wales, where he hoped to rally as much support as he could. He often fell into long hours of brooding, fearful of the future, and wondering in particular how he could make sure the Red Knight would support him in the war with Galehaut. He drew confidence from his nephew's improvement – the threat of death had passed – but even when his wounds had healed, it seemed clear that Gawain would prove no substitute for the unidentified knight. Arthur asked him to organize a search. Forty knights – Sir Yvain, Kay the Seneschal, Sir Gawain himself, as well as his brothers and other valiant members of the king's household – would go out in quest of the Red Knight, taking all the time they needed until the end of the truce.

¶ No one imagined that the White Knight who had conquered Dolorous Guard, and whose name and parentage were still unknown, had evolved into the Red Knight they were seeking. He had gone from the battlefield back to Malehaut, in greater need of convalescence than before.

He had come in very quietly during the night, and the servants who were waiting for him removed his armor. He was so badly hurt, so exhausted, that he wanted only to sleep and would take nothing to eat. Word came to the chatelaine that the battle had been won by a knight of extraordinary prowess, whose shield was red. Suspecting it had been her mysterious guest, she went to look at his horse, who was standing before his full manger with wounds all over him. The knight's armor, too, gave proof of heroic encounters – it seemed astonishing that he was still alive! The lady was even more surprised when she saw the knight himself, sound asleep, covered with a blanket except for his face and arms, which were swollen, bruised, and encrusted with blood. Only the greatest of warriors, she thought, could have endured so much. It seemed to her that a great love must have inspired him.

Blaye went to Carduel, where the king and queen welcomed her warmly. She was one of the noblest ladies in the realm, and had often sent Arthur reinforcements when he needed them. Knowing that she seldom left her lands, the king asked why she had done so now.

"Ah, my lord," she replied, "an envious neighbor has voiced against my dear late father's sister accusations that are unjust and cannot be left unanswered. She is in need of a champion to defend her rights, and it was my hope that it could be the knight who fought so valiantly on your behalf a little while ago – the one you call the Red Knight."

The king told her that forty of his men were even then searching for that very knight, and no one had any idea where he was. "In that case," said the lady, "one of my own knights will have to do." But she smiled to herself, since now she was certain that her guest was indeed the mysterious hero.

She returned home quickly, eager to see again the knight who could inspire so many others to distinguish themselves in combat. She was proud to have him under her roof, and she was charmed by the secret of it all. Though still ignorant of his identity and his motives, she was satisfied that others knew even less.

During her absence, the Lady of Malehaut's doctor had visited the knight at her request. He had done what he could to speed the healing of the young man's wounds, but insisted that rest, at least until the chatelaine returned, was absolutely necessary. At that time, even though he was still weak from loss of blood, the Red Knight insisted on leaving. Blaye had to allow it, but she made him promise to come back before the second battle with the Lord of the Distant Isles. Lancelot gave his word, adding that he was at her service if ever she had need of him.

℘ During the truce, King Arthur, mindful of his distressing dreams, tried hard to follow the advice of his wise men. He bent every effort to win back the affection of his people, traveling to all the cities of his realm, settling complaints of injustice, attentive to the troubles of those less fortunate than others. Wherever he went, he invited the local knights to splendid feasts, treating them with great courtesy and doing them honor in every way he could. He gave precious gifts to everyone, rare luxuries to the great lords, more practical things to the needy, sometimes even the horse that he himself was riding. The queen, for her part, was unstinting in her kindness toward the women and girls of the kingdom. Little by little, such generosity turned the apathy of Arthur's subjects to love. By the end of the year, a multitude of knights were ready to fight for the king's honor, understanding now how much they had at stake in his victory.

Arthur was reassured by this, and also by the forty knights' return from their quest a few weeks before the end of the truce. His pleasure was more than offset, however, by their failure to find any trace of the Red Knight, for now he would have to confront Galehaut without the unknown champion. But he succeeded in hiding his disappointment – indeed his distress – from Sir Gawain and the others, lest he dishearten or offend them. They set out right away for the second, and crucial, encounter with Arthur's great challenger.

WHEN LANCELOT LEFT MALEHAUT, the Red Knight disappeared forever. Carrying only a plain shield with no identifying insignia, the Lord of Joyous Guard set out for his own domain, there to enjoy the pleasures of rulership and to recover the rest of his strength. But Lancelot could not be idle for long. Soon he was riding over the countryside in search of little adventures to occupy his time before the tremendous challenge that lay ahead. No incident along the way, however, could distract him from the thought of the conflict looming between King Arthur and the man intent on capturing his realm. It called to Lancelot with the promise of new renown and significant service to the queen. He nevertheless resolved to be very sure he was needed before entering the field. He returned to Malehaut in good time for the battle.

❦ By the appointed day, the Lord of the Distant Isles had assembled twice as many men as before. The iron nets could no longer encircle their camp. Two thousand of Arthur's men did battle with three thousand of Galehaut's, and it seemed that the smaller battalions had the advantage. But Galehaut, seeing this, sent so many into the field that despite extraordinary efforts, Arthur's knights realized there was no hope they could ultimately prevail. Sir Gawain, as before, performed wondrous feats of arms, his example giving courage to those around him, but for every two of Arthur's men there were three of Galehaut's. Then, when Gawain's horse was killed under him and he himself was terribly wounded, Arthur sent in all the knights he had left. Sir Yvain, leading the reinforcements, knocked the First Defeated King off his horse and helped Gawain to remount. In the very grip of death, Gawain fought on. When darkness stopped the battle, he was found still on horseback, but bleeding from mouth and nose, unable to speak. He was carried to Arthur's tent, where he collapsed, unconscious. Everyone believed that this time he would surely die. The king and queen despaired, and the doctors dared not reveal their true opinion. There was consternation throughout Arthur's camp; knights wept and said that no nobler man could ever perish.

The dire news soon reached Malehaut. It was far worse than Lancelot had expected, and he reproached himself for not having joined the battle at the start. "How could I not have thought that something like this might happen?" he lamented. "I should have been there! If Sir Gawain dies, the kingdom will never recover from the loss."

He ran to tell Blaye that he must leave immediately, and was angered to hear that the new armor she had promised him was not yet ready. "When you offered to equip me, you said there would be no delay! I must be ready to fight if summoned to do so. It may already be too late!"

"Perhaps you would care," she said, seizing her opportunity, "to tell me who you are. If I at least knew your name, I could feel better disposed toward you."

The knight stared at her with wet eyes and offered no answer. She went on, "No name – and all your readiness to show your valor in the field, if summoned. What can I suspect but that some uncommon love drives you on?"

"My lady," he said, restraining himself at every word, "you have been most generous to me, and I am forever in your debt. But it would shame me to bargain for what I need."

The chatelaine knew the value of patience. She simply replied that the fighting would not, in any case, resume for two more days. By that time his new armor, black, like his warhorse, would be ready. She herself would go directly to King Arthur's camp, but she asked the knight not to leave her castle until it was time for the battle. Lancelot reluctantly agreed.

℘ The morning of the battle, the Lady of Malehaut was with the king and queen and Gawain, somewhat recovered but still not out of danger, in a wooden gallery overlooking the field. A knight in black armor appeared below, standing near the ford and leaning on his lance. Blaye knew him at once; Sir Gawain thought there was something about his stance that suggested the Red Knight. The lady proposed that the queen send a message, urging the knight to join the fighting, but Guenevere declined to do so. With the king at risk of losing his lands and honor, and her nephew badly wounded, she could not give any thought to the quite uncertain help of an unknown spectator.

The Lady of Malehaut herself, and other ladies present, decided to send the knight their own message, saying that they all – even without the explicit assent of the queen – implored him to do his best for the love of them and for the king.

A maiden rode off to speak to the knight, followed by a squire who carried two lances, a gift from Sir Gawain. The Black Knight thanked her courteously, asked the squire to follow him, and settled himself in his stirrups. Gawain, watching from the gallery, had the impression that he grew half a foot taller as he readied himself for combat. The knight looked up toward the spectators, turned and galloped into the field, racing past jousting knights and larger melees until a whole battalion was coming toward him. Then his lance struck an enemy knight such a blow that man and horse fell together to the ground.

The Black Knight fought until his weapon was worn down to the grip. Then he quickly seized the first gift lance from the squire, and after that the second. His skill was so great that many stopped fighting to watch him in amazement, but when he had used all his lances he left the field and returned to the edge of the ford, where he stood once more gazing at the gallery. Sir Gawain said to the queen, "That is the greatest knight in all the world. You were wrong not to ask for his help – he must have thought you were too proud to do so. But he is our only hope."

The Lady of Malehaut added, "It's clear he won't do anything more for us!"

The queen asked Gawain what he thought she should say.

"Send your greetings to him, and ask him, of his grace, to defend the kingdom of Logres, and to accomplish such feats of arms as would deserve your gratitude. I myself will send him ten sharp, strong lances and three of my best horses."

When the Black Knight received this message, he replied, "Please say to my lady that everything shall be as she desires, and tell Sir Gawain I am grateful for his gift."

Then he rode into the fray, passing countless jousts and duels and melees until he came to the First Defeated King's battalion with its two thousand knights. He charged right through them as fast as the horse could go, wielding his lance so perfectly that the ground behind him was littered with fallen men and horses. King Arthur's knights watched in astonishment. Sir Kay the Seneschal, Sagremor the Unruly, Do's son Girflet, Sir Yvain, Brandeliz, and Sir Gawain's brother Gaheriet were awe-struck. Kay said, "My lords, you have just seen the most magnificent charge ever made by a knight. If we want to win honor today, we won't let him fight all alone. I'd be glad of your company, but with or without it I won't leave his side as long as there's life left in me."

At that he spurred his horse, and the others instantly followed. The knight in black armor had stopped fighting just long enough to seize another lance, and was galloping back. The six knights rode up on either side of him, and all of them together struck blow after blow where the opposing forces were thickest. Arthur's knights and Galehaut's watched the

Black Knight with equal wonder. They recalled the Red Knight of the year before and found the Black Knight even more remarkable. Soon he had used up all his lances, and one of Gawain's horses fell dead beneath him. The squire brought another to where the knight was standing on the field, and he leapt onto its back and began to fight again, sword in hand. He seemed as fresh as if the battle had only just begun.

No one came against the Black Knight without being un-horsed. His six companions did their best to keep up with him, inspired by his example. He began to find the way open before him. Galehaut's men thought they could not outdo those who had faced the Black Knight already; their armor had protected them no better than naked skin. Meanwhile the battalion led by the King of the Hundred Knights was re-treating before King Yder. But driven into the First Defeated King's battalion, they turned around and, together with their allies, began again to prevail. The field was crowded with bat-tling men and fierce melees; knights lay dead and dying every-where, and frantic horses galloped riderless. Yet in both armies they talked of nothing but the Black Knight, and Galehaut went to see the one who was "winning the war all by himself!"

Again the Black Knight's horse was killed under him. His six companions began to fare less well, and Sir Kay sent an urgent message to Hervi de Rivel, who, with banners flying, arrived with reinforcements, although he was well over eighty years old. By noon there were four battalions on each side, but in Galehaut's there were two thousand more men. And these

would have made all the difference, had it not been for the
Black Knight, whose prowess gave strength to those on
Arthur's side and disheartened the enemy. When Galehaut
saw his knights running shamefully back to their camp, he
led a large company to turn them around. In his presence, his
knights recovered their confidence and began shouting
his battle cry.

The fighting became even fiercer, but still the Black Knight
managed to prevent the rout of Arthur's army. Then his last
horse was killed, and the fighting was so thick around him
that the squire could not get through. On foot now, like a war
flag fixed in the ground, his sword slashing left and right, he
was soon surrounded by dead and wounded knights, their
helmets broken, their shields in pieces, their chain mail in
tatters, arms cut off at the shoulder. Galehaut, watching in
wonder, thought that no kingdom he might ever conquer
could be worth the life of such a knight. His skill was matchless; he was superb, as invincible as any man could be. Galehaut spurred his horse through the press, forcing his men to
give way and stand back.

Thus there came to be a lull in the fighting, and in the
silence the Black Knight saw approaching him a warrior taller
than any on the field. He was wearing armor that shone golden
in the sunlight and was riding a red-gold charger that carried
him with ease. There was such majesty about him that the
young knight knew he was in the presence of a king as he had
dreamed a king might be, a ruler even more regal than King

Arthur. Galehaut's voice, too, deep and clear, expressed an absolute authority, and with it, solicitude: "Sir, do not be afraid."

"Nor am I," was the reply.

"Let me tell you what I intend. Not one of my men will raise a hand against you as long as you are on foot. You shall not be taken prisoner unless you try to leave the field. My squire will bring you a new horse. If that one is killed, you shall have another, no matter how many you need. If I can't wear you out, then no one ever will!"

So the Black Knight, freshly mounted, began fighting again as if he had not struck a single blow the whole day. Galehaut rejoined his troops, ordering one thousand men to attack immediately, "and you," he said to his liege man King Bademagus, "will wait until every last man on the other side has begun to fight – I'll bring you word. They will think all my troops are already in the field."

To have the horsemen appear more numerous, he had them spread out as much as possible, and when they were close to the battle, the sound of their horns and trumpets shook the ground. The Black Knight gathered King Arthur's men around him and said, "My lords, I don't know all your names, but I know that you are thought to be most valiant. Now we will see how well you deserve your reputations."

Sir Yvain, confident that Galehaut's whole army was on the field, said, "From the looks of them there's no way for us to lose!" But Gawain, who had a better view, realized that only a portion of Galehaut's forces had arrived. These knights attacked with such energy that many of Arthur's were killed in their first charge. But Yvain rallied the others to such effect that Galehaut rode back to where his reserves were concealed, and ordered them to "ride as you have never ridden before! Strike down every one of them! You have done nothing here but rest and preserve your strength. Now is your chance to use it."

King Arthur's knights had nearly put Galehaut's to rout, thanks to the valiant efforts of Yvain — and his feats of arms were as nothing compared with those of the Black Knight. They could do little, however, against Galehaut's fresh battalion, and the Black Knight, like the six companions who had fought at his side all day, was soon unhorsed. Galehaut's squire was there in an instant, bringing another mount, and the Black Knight galloped back into the melee. All afternoon he fought so brilliantly that Galehaut thought no man had ever shown such courage or such skill.

℄ When dusk brought an end to the fighting, the Black Knight slipped away as quietly as he could, riding through the meadow between the hillside and the river. But Galehaut saw him go, and spurring his horse, followed him for a moment, then rode up beside him. In the lordly presence of this man, unlike any other he had seen, the Black Knight felt his own youth. But Galehaut said only, "God be with you, good sir!" The knight glanced at him and returned his greeting, though not without a moment's hesitation. Galehaut asked, "Who are you?"

"My lord, I am a knight, as you can see."

"Indeed you are, the best in the world, and I honor you for that. I have never seen an invincible knight until now. I would like to know you better and hope you will agree to be my guest this evening. I am Galehaut, the son of the Giantess and ruler of all those noble lords you have fought in defense of Logres. If not for you, that kingdom would now be in my power."

"How is it that King Arthur's enemy cares to give me hospitality? God forbid that I should accept it!"

"I have already shown my friendship for you on the battlefield, and I trust that is only the beginning. Once you have been my guest, you may ask of me anything at all, and I will not refuse."

At that the Black Knight stopped his horse and looked hard at Galehaut: "You are known as a man of honor, my lord. I think you would not make such an offer unless in good faith."

"You may be sure of that! You shall have from me whatever you desire, if I can have your company tonight. Indeed, I would gladly have it for longer."

"Will you swear to this in the presence of the two men you trust the most?"

Galehaut said he would do so. "Will you now tell me who you are?"

"I am Lancelot of the Lake, son of King Ban of Benoic."

"So the son of King Ban is fighting for King Arthur?"

Lancelot was puzzled by Galehaut's surprise. "What do you mean?"

"Don't you know that your father lost his kingdom because Arthur had no time to come to his help?"

Lancelot was too startled to respond immediately. Then he said, "I fight with a sword that was given to me by the queen."

℘ From his vantage point, Gawain had seen the Black Knight leaving the field with Galehaut. He called to the queen, who was close by, and sent someone in haste to find the king. They saw how Galehaut had his hand on the Black Knight's shoulder, and watched as the two men slowly rode where Arthur's troops would have to see them. Gawain spoke bitterly to the king, reproaching him for the unworthiness which, as his wise men had predicted, was clearly exacting a high price. Was it not costing him the loyalty of the one knight who could have saved his kingdom? "All day long he fought for your honor and your lands, and now you have let him go with no thanks from you! Look what your foe has had the wisdom to win! Galehaut will better know how to value his service!" Gawain was in anguish as he spoke. "Your time has come, my lord, for you see what a treasure you are losing!"

Weeping, the king offered his nephew what little comfort he could. The queen was in such despair she could not speak. Arthur retired to his quarters to grieve for his fate, and, as the news spread, no one in his army failed to lament their now inevitable defeat. Without the Black Knight they would quickly be overrun by Galehaut's forces, and the Lord of the Distant Isles would take Arthur's place as the ruler of Logres.

℘ At Galehaut's camp, the King of the Hundred Knights and the First Defeated King were summoned to join their liege lord. They were delighted to see the Black Knight in their midst, but objected when Galehaut asked them to witness an unconditional pledge. He told them, sharply, "Don't try to change my mind! I know very well what I am doing. I have also agreed that should I break my promise, you will both renounce your fealty to me, and give him your allegiance instead." They were reluctant but said they would do as he wished.

Then Galehaut drew the First Defeated King aside: "Go to all my liege men and ask them to come to my tent in their most splendid attire. Tell them that I have accomplished something wonderful, and want to have a great celebration."

Cleolas went to do his bidding, while Galehaut and the King of the Hundred Knights kept the Black Knight in conversation until everything was made ready. Before long, two hundred knights were gathered before Galehaut's pavilion, all of them his vassals, with thirty kings among them, along with dukes and counts and barons. They gave the Black Knight a warmly enthusiastic welcome, calling him, to his great embarrassment, "the flower of knighthood." His armor was replaced by a sumptuous silken robe that Galehaut pressed upon him. The festivities that evening at Galehaut's pavilion were beyond telling; jongleurs had already learned new songs of victory, and the meal of game and river fish, of cider, ale, and wine, would not be soon forgotten.

When it was time to rest, the Black Knight was led to a chamber in which there were four beds. The largest of these was draped in silk and piled high with furs and soft pillows; this bed, Galehaut insisted, would be for his guest, and the other three for servants. He himself would spend the night in another tent. Thinking of the noble welcome he had been given, and with great esteem for Galehaut in his heart, the knight was soon fast asleep. Then, accompanied by two other knights, Galehaut came in and very quietly lay down next to him. He stayed awake through the night, watching the young man rest and dream, listening to his steady breathing, but puzzled time and again to hear him moaning in his sleep. Galehaut wondered what might be the cause of such great sadness, but for him, filled with admiration and affection, the overriding question was how to keep the Black Knight by his side. He left the chamber at dawn, before his guest could be aware of his presence.

That morning after mass, the Black Knight asked for his armor. "Dear friend," said Galehaut, "tell me how I can persuade you to stay longer. There is nothing I wouldn't do. You may well meet men more powerful than I am, but never one who cares for you as much. And since I would do the most to have you with me, I can claim to be the one you should be with!"

"There is no one, my lord, whose friendship I would prefer to yours, and I will stay with you gladly, but only if you grant me what I am about to ask."

"If it is within my power, you shall have it."

The knight asked the two kings who had witnessed Galehaut's oath to come forward. Then he said, "My lord, when
you have won your war with King Arthur, leaving him no
recourse but to declare himself defeated, and when I tell you
that the time has come, you must go to him and ask for
mercy, putting yourself in his power."

No one could have foreseen such a request. Galehaut was
too astonished to speak, and the two kings looked at each
other as if seeking confirmation of what they had just heard.
In the silence, one of them protested: "What are you waiting
for, my lord? You have gone so far you can't turn back now!"

"Do you think I am sorry I made that promise? If the
world were mine to give, he should have it gladly! I was overcome by the beauty of his words, for no one has ever understood friendship so well. Good sir, may God turn away from
me if I fail to grant your wish! You could ask nothing of me
that would be to my dishonor. I ask you in return not to
deprive me of your company."

And so the knight stayed on. They all went to have a festive
meal, Galehaut's army celebrating the Black Knight's presence
in their midst, while those in Arthur's camp, not knowing the
agreement that had been made, lamented bitterly.

℘ The next morning, Galehaut asked his guest if he would
join them on the field. "Gladly," was the reply, and he also
agreed to wear Galehaut's own armor, except for the coat of

mail and greaves which were too large. The men on both sides prepared for battle. King Arthur said that no one was to cross the river before he gave the order, but nothing could restrain the younger knights, and soon there were jousts here and there on the field, and then melees, and finally both armies were fully engaged. King Arthur stood by his standard with four trusted knights who were to escort the queen to safety should things go badly.

A knight rode out into the field, and those on Arthur's side recognized Galehaut's armor. But Gawain, who had a keener eye, shouted, "No! That's the Black Knight!" The cry demoralized the king's army, and his men began to flee, with Galehaut's much greater forces close behind them. The Black Knight, however, stood between the two armies and allowed King Arthur's men to make good their retreat. When they were safely inside their own lines, he called to Galehaut, who spurred his horse and was instantly at his side, saying, "What do you wish, my friend?"

"Something impossible."

"Just tell me."

"My lord, would you say you have won?"

"Without a doubt."

"Then it is time to fulfill your promise."

"And so I will."

When the Black Knight saw that Galehaut was willing, for his sake, to make such a sacrifice, he knew that he could never find a better, truer, friend. Tears ran down his face, and he murmured, "Dear God, could anyone be worthy of this?"

Galehaut was galloping straight toward the king, who stood near his standard, ready to die with the shame of his defeat. For Arthur, all hope was lost. The queen was already riding away with her escort. They had wanted to carry Gawain on a stretcher, but he refused, saying that he preferred death to the loss of all joy and honor. He fell unconscious, and it seemed that he was indeed very near his end.

Galehaut rode up to the royal standard, and asked to speak with the king. As Arthur came toward him, believing that he was about to lose all the honor he had in the world, Galehaut dismounted and, kneeling on the ground with the palms of his hands pressed together, said, "My lord, I repent the wrong I have done you. I have come to make amends, and to place myself entirely at your mercy."

Surprise and relief flooded the king's heart at these words, and he raised his hands toward heaven. Could he believe what he had just heard? He replied hesitantly and humbly, asking the Lord of the Distant Isles, the very image of chivalric honor, to rise. The two men embraced. Galehaut said, "My lord, I am yours to do with as you will. With your permission, I will order my men to withdraw. Then I'll come back to you."

"Do so, and return as soon as you can. We have much to speak about."

While Galehaut attended to this, the king sent messengers on fast horses to bring back the queen. Once she was convinced that their report was true, she felt overwhelmed with relief and happiness. The king went himself to tell Gawain, who, shocked back into full consciousness, asked, "My lord, how can this have happened?"

"I have no idea, except that it must have been God's will to save us."

Galehaut went to the Black Knight and said, "My friend, what is your pleasure? I have done as you asked. Shall we return to the king now?"

"My lord, let the king enjoy your company alone! What you have done today is far more than I could ever deserve. But I must beg you not to tell anyone where I am."

Galehaut agreed, and they rode on toward their tents. Word spread through the army of how the peace had been made, but many were discontent, as they would have preferred the excitement and danger of war.

¶ The two companions disarmed, and Galehaut put on his most splendid robes to wear to court. He gave his knights permission to return to their homes if they wished, except those of his own household. Then he summoned the two kings, in whom he had absolute confidence, and asked them to take good care of the Black Knight, who was his friend and should be treated as if he were Galehaut himself.

When the Lord of the Distant Isles arrived at court, King Arthur, disarmed as well, came to welcome him. The queen was there too, as were Blaye and other ladies. They went to the gallery where Gawain was lying, and, weak as he was, the king's nephew greeted Galehaut warmly, saying that he had wanted to meet him and aspired to have his friendship, since "no one in the world is so worthy of esteem, so greatly loved by his people, and so capable of recognizing true nobility – as you have just now so clearly shown us." When Galehaut inquired about his health, Gawain replied, "I was very close to death, my lord, but now I am fully restored by the joy and love that, by God's grace, you have come to share with the king. No one could be in good health as long as there was enmity between the two worthiest men on earth!"

Galehaut spent the whole day with the king and queen and Gawain. They spoke of many things, but the Black Knight was never mentioned. They shared a tacit understanding that it would be indelicate to touch on the strange behavior of that mysterious figure. Their curiosity could wait for another time.

⊄ Toward evening, Galehaut asked leave to go and see his men. King Arthur allowed it, on condition that he return before long. Galehaut told this to his friend as soon as he saw him, "but I don't want to be where you are not. You are dearer to me than everything I have aspired to in the world."

Then the knight asked the state of things at court but said nothing about the queen. Galehaut spoke of the courteous welcome he had received, especially from Gawain, and, as for Guenevere, "no woman who ever lived could be her equal."

Hearing Galehaut utter such words about the queen, the knight bowed his head and was lost in thought. Galehaut, surprised to see tears in his eyes, began to speak of other things. At last the knight said, "I think you should go keep the king and Sir Gawain company. If anyone speaks of me, remember what they say so you can tell me about it tomorrow."

"Of course I will," said Galehaut, embracing his friend and commending him to God. He told the two kings that the knight was dearer to him "than the very heart in my breast," and to take care of him accordingly. Galehaut slept that night in Arthur's pavilion; Yvain and other knights were there too, and Gawain was brought in on a stretcher. The queen and her ladies retired to her chamber, together with the Lady of Malehaut, always alert for what she might learn.

℧ The Black Knight, in Galehaut's camp with the two kings, was treated with such deference that he felt quite embarrassed. They spent the night close to him, as Galehaut had done, without his knowing it. At first the young man slept quietly, but soon he began to toss and turn, groaning so loudly that he woke his two companions. Over and over again they heard him murmur, "Alas! What can I do?"

Although the two kings rose very early the next morning, Galehaut had already arrived, curious to know how things were with his friend. They told him about the sounds of distress they had heard, and Galehaut, remembering a similar occasion, went straight to the bed chamber. The knight, hearing his footsteps, dried his eyes and lay very still so that he seemed to be asleep. When he arose, a little later, he tried to be cheerful. His eyes were still red, however, and his voice so hoarse he could hardly speak.

Galehaut asked, "My dear friend, please tell me what makes you so sad. No matter how terrible it is, let me try to help you." At that the knight began to weep again, as if all that he loved in the world lay dead at his feet. Galehaut took him in his arms, cradling his head and comforting him as best he could, imploring him to speak about his grief, "and if anyone has wronged you, whoever it may be, you will surely be avenged."

"No one has wronged me in any way."

"Are you unhappy to have let me make you my lord and my companion?"

"You have done much more for me than I could ever deserve –" he paused, "but there is a terrible fear in my heart that I may die because of your kindness."

Greatly troubled, Galehaut tried his best to give his friend confidence, swearing that he would never do anything to harm or distress him and would search the world to obtain for him whatever he might desire.

❡ When Galehaut was at court again, he went with the king and queen to visit Gawain, who could no longer contain his curiosity. "I hope you will not mind if I ask you something. May we know who arranged the peace between you and my king?"

"Was he wearing black armor?" interrupted the queen. "We saw him leave the field in your company, and he wore your armor yesterday."

"That is true. But I can tell you no more about him than you already know. Have you ever seen a man more valiant than he?"

"Never," said the king, "not even the Red Knight, whose valor made me so greatly desire to know him."

"Then what would you give to have him with you always?"

"I would give him half of all I possess. Except my queen, of course!"

Then Galehaut asked Gawain what he would give, if he had his health again, to have the Black Knight as his companion. Gawain hesitated, wondering if his wounds would ever heal, and then replied that he would willingly be transformed into a beautiful young woman, if he could have the Black Knight's love his whole life long.

"And you, my lady?" Galehaut asked the queen.

"Now that Gawain has offered all that a lady can give, a lady can do no more!"

With that, they all laughed, but Galehaut, when they demanded that he too answer the question, said that for the love of that knight, "I would let my very honor turn to shame."

"God knows," said Gawain, "that you have offered more than any of us." He realized that Galehaut had actually done what he said: at the very moment when he had won the war, he had given his triumph away. He pointed this out to the queen, and Galehaut was more esteemed than ever. There was much talk of the Black Knight, and then the queen asked Galehaut to escort her to her quarters.

On the way she spoke to him in confidence, saying that she was very fond of him and adding, "I know that the Black Knight is in your power. If you value my love at all, make it possible for me to see him. I would be forever in your debt."

"My lady, I have no power over him, and I haven't seen him myself since the peace was arranged."

"But surely you know where he is!"

"I think he has gone to my home. And of course I will do my best to find him for you."

"In that case, it can't be long before he is here, and I thank you with all my heart. Let your messengers ride night and day!"

Galehaut returned to the king, who suggested that since their armies had been dispersed, leaving only their own households, the two camps should be brought closer to each other. "My lord, I will have all our tents set up at the river's edge, with my own set across from yours. A boat will be made ready to go from one side to the other. I'll attend to that right away."

⁋ The Black Knight laughed to hear what the king and Gawain had said they would do to have his company, and he heartily approved the king's idea of bringing the two camps closer to each other. As soon as Galehaut touched on the queen's desire to see him, however, his smile vanished. He made no reply, and his eyes filled with tears. Galehaut said, "Don't be distressed, but say what you want me to do. I'd rather have half the world angry with me than you alone – if I care about anyone else at all, it's only because of you."

"From now on, I will do whatever you advise."

"I don't think," Galehaut suggested, "that seeing the queen could be harmful to anyone."

"For me it will be joy and suffering."

Then Galehaut understood what was in the knight's heart, and pressed him so hard that Lancelot agreed the time had come – "only no one else must know. Tell my lady that you have sent for me."

Galehaut called his seneschal and ordered him to have the entire camp brought to the river's edge, directly across from the king's encampment. Then, with a few attendants, he went to court, where the queen came in haste to meet him. In answer to her question he said, "My lady, I have done your bidding, and now I stand to lose what I love more than anything else in the world."

"Should my service ever cost you anything, I will give it back twice over. But what could you possibly lose?"

"The very man you are asking for."

"You're right," she said. "I could never make good such a loss, but, God willing, you will not lose him through my fault." Impatient with this turn in the conversation, she simply went on. "When will he come?"

"I told my messengers to make all speed."

"Then it could be tomorrow."

"Not even if he started out right now – though I too wish he were here already!"

❖   ❖   ❖

℘ While they were talking, Galehaut's many-colored tents were moved close to the river, where people kept coming to look at them. They marveled at the splendor of the ornate pavilions and, fluttering along the water's edge, the pennons and ensigns of the Lord of the Distant Isles and his allies.

Galehaut went back to be with his friend, and told him how the queen was impatient to see him, which filled the knight's heart with joy and apprehension. They spoke for a long time, and then Galehaut returned to court, where Guenevere asked if he had any news for her. "Not yet," he replied.

"My friend, I think you are putting off what you could hasten."

"My desire to see him is surely as strong as yours."

"That's exactly what I fear. Sometimes people refuse things just because they like them so much themselves. But there is nothing for you to be concerned about – you will never lose what you have because of me."

"I thank you for that, my lady – soon you'll be able to help me far more than I can help you."

That night the king insisted that Galehaut sleep in his pavilion, but early the next morning he returned to his friend and told him what the queen had said. The knight was beginning to feel more confident; there was color in his cheeks, and his eyes no longer showed signs of weeping. Happy to see him looking much more like himself, Galehaut asked how he should reply to the queen. "I am sure she will expect to see you tomorrow, and I hope you will agree."

"I wish that day had already come and gone!"

Galehaut saw his friend was agitated and vacillating, eager to respond to the queen's summons but worried at the same time. Saying nothing further, Galehaut went to the king's tent where the queen, as before, asked if he had any news. "My lady, it is still too soon, but we should hear something by tomorrow."

"I think it is in your power to make it sooner rather than later. Pray do me the kindness you would hope to receive from me were the situation reversed."

Galehaut laughed, and Blaye, who had overheard every word and thought she knew what they were speaking about, was determined to find out more.

The next morning Galehaut told his companion that truly he could delay no longer. The knight replied, "But I beg you to make sure I can come and go unseen."

"Have no fear." Galehaut left the tent and called his seneschal. "If I send for you, bring the Black Knight with you, and let no one be aware of what you are doing."

"As you wish, my lord."

GALEHAUT WENT TO THE KING'S
pavilion and gave the queen some welcome news:
"The flower of all knighthood is here at last!"

"How can I see him? No one must know about
this except the three of us."

"He said the same thing – he doesn't want to be seen by
anyone from the king's household."

"I don't know who the Black Knight is, and I'm all the more
impatient."

"It won't be long, my lady." He gazed outside, considering
the landscape. "We'll go for a walk in the meadow over there, as
discreetly as we can, and just before nightfall he will be there."

"If only God would make it turn dark right now!" They
both laughed at that, and the queen gave Galehaut a cheerful
embrace. The Lady of Malehaut, seeing this, thought that
something must be about to happen and looked carefully at
every knight who came along. Guenevere spent the day in
conversation and pastimes to make the hours go more quickly.
After supper she took Galehaut by the hand and, accompanied by Blaye and two others, began her stroll through the
meadow. Galehaut sent a squire to his seneschal with a message to meet him there in a certain secluded place.

⊄ They came to a grove of apple trees, and Galehaut sat down with the queen, somewhat apart from the others. The evening sky was darkening, but there were no clouds and the moon was full. Meanwhile the seneschal had crossed the river. He and the knight were both such handsome men that when they came into view, and Galehaut told the queen that this was "the best knight in the world," she wondered which one he meant. Dressed in simple tunics, neither seemed to her likely to possess the valor of the Black Knight. Galehaut assured her that he was one of the two. Blaye, however, had immediately recognized her former guest, and she hid her face as he passed. The queen, then, was the object of his love, the lady he had been so reluctant to name! Blaye found consolation for her lost hopes in the knowledge that she could never rival Guenevere. There was a certain comfort, too, in simply finding an answer to her question.

Then the two men were in the presence of the queen. The seneschal bowed to her and the other ladies, but the knight was trembling so hard that he could scarcely move. He kept his eyes fixed on the ground as if deeply embarrassed; he was very pale. The queen realized that he must be the one. Galehaut told the seneschal to go keep the other ladies company. Then the queen took the knight by the hand, and had him sit beside her. She smiled at him graciously and said, "My lord, we have had such a great desire to see you, and now, thanks to God and to Galehaut here, we have the joy of doing so. And yet I do not know whether you really are the knight I have been asking for, and I hope you will be pleased to tell me yourself."

He murmured, without raising his eyes, that he didn't know. The queen was surprised, and began to suspect what was troubling him. Thinking the knight might be less tongue-tied if no one else were there, Galehaut went to join the seneschal, declaring that it was not proper for several ladies to be accompanied by only one knight. Soon they were all involved in conversation.

The queen spoke to the knight: "Good sir, why have you been so unwilling to let us know who you are? What possible reason could there be? At least you can tell me this: was it you who won the battle the day before yesterday?"

"No, my lady."

"What! Weren't you the knight in black armor? Wasn't it to you that Gawain sent three horses?"

"Yes, my lady."

"Then on the last day, weren't you wearing Galehaut's armor?"

"Yes, my lady."

"And weren't you the winner on the first and second days?"

"No – that was someone else."

Not to take credit for his victories seemed admirable to the queen. "Who was it that made you a knight?"

"You did, my lady."

"I did?"

73

"Do you remember the boy who came to King Arthur's court on a Friday and became a knight that Sunday, which was the Feast of Saint John?"

"I remember very well. The Lady of the Lake presented him to the king, dressed all in white. Was that you?"

"Yes, my lady."

"Then why do you say that I made you a knight?"

"Because it is true. The one who makes a man a knight is the person who gives him his sword, and mine did not come from the king. It came from you."

"When was that?"

"Do you not remember a knight who once brought two maidens to see you? He told you that they had been rescued from great peril by a man in white armor who considered himself your knight. Since he had not received a sword from the king, he asked that you send him one. And you did. It is the sword I have used ever since."

"Are you the White Knight who achieved the Adventure of Dolorous Guard and undid all the enchantments of the castle? Was it you who fought off a whole army to have Gawain and his companions released from prison?"

"I knew that they needed help."

"The Lady of the Lake brought you to Camelot to be knighted, but I still don't know who you are. Please tell me."

There was a long silence. "I am Lancelot," he answered, "the son of Ban of Benoic."

The queen drew a sharp breath as she recalled Arthur's

failure to help the father under siege. And now King Ban's son was sitting beside her! But she said only, "Many have done knightly deeds, but yours are so astonishing that I can only wonder what inspires you."

"My lady, whatever I have done was only for you."

"For me?"

"I love you more than myself, more than anyone or anything in the world."

"But I have spoken to you just twice before, when you first arrived at court and when you were leaving."

"That was when I came to you in my armor, and told you that wherever I went in the world I would be your knight. And you accepted my service, and I took leave of you, and you said 'Farewell, dear friend.' Those words have never left my heart. They have made me a worthy knight, if I really am one. They have saved me from every evil and every danger. They comforted me whenever I was sad. They fed me when I was hungry. They make me rich in my great poverty."

"Then God be praised that I spoke them! I am glad you understood me as you did, and gained so much by that." She paused a moment, then said with a delicate reluctance, "But in truth I have said as much to many knights, without meaning anything special."

℺ The knight could hardly grasp the sense behind these words, but he felt their impact in the very core of his being. All the blood rushed from his head, and he would have fallen had the queen not caught him by the shoulder. Frightened, she called to Galehaut who came running and asked what had happened. "You might have killed him!" he exclaimed. The knight was barely conscious.

"Did you know that he was the victor at Dolorous Guard? That he was the one who rescued Gawain from prison? That he was also the Red Knight and the Black Knight? And all his noble deeds, if I can believe him, were just for the love of me! Because I called him 'dear friend,' he thought that I loved him!"

The novelty of the situation and the naïveté of the knight brought ripples of excited pleasure into the queen's voice. Galehaut was far less buoyant in his response.

"Ah, my lady, you can believe him! Just as he is more valiant than other men, his heart is truer. When you wanted help, I did what I could for you, and now I am asking you to take pity on him! I know, beyond a doubt, that he loves you more than anything else in the world, and no man has ever done more for a lady. Remember that the peace I made with the king was entirely due to this knight."

At this, a hint of gravity appeared in the queen's words too. "Had he done no more than that, I would be forever in his debt, and I owe you much as well. I am certainly inclined to listen to him favorably – but he hasn't asked me for anything!"

"He wouldn't dare! At his age, there can be no love without fear, so he did not have the courage to make the slightest request. It was only from the sorrow he couldn't conceal that

I came to know how much he loves you. That's why I am speaking for him," and he added, "although you shouldn't need me to tell you that to win the love of this man is to have won the finest treasure the world can offer."

"Tell me what I should do."

"Grant him your love; be loyal to him for all the years of your life. There could be no greater gift."

She considered the bluntness of this statement, and its implications, for a long moment. Then, with an intensity almost matching Galehaut's, she said, "I solemnly promise that my love will be entirely his, as his is entirely mine, and we will depend on you to help us solve any problems."

"Thank you, my lady. And now will you give him a pledge of your commitment?"

"With all my heart."

"Then I think you should kiss him."

"Not here — those ladies, who must already wonder what is happening, can't fail to see us. But just the same, if he wants me to, I will gladly do as you say." They spoke as if the subject of their discussion were not present.

But now the knight, overwhelmed by conflicting emotions, murmured, "My lady, I thank you."

Galehaut said, "If we put our heads together as if we were making plans, no one will see anything."

The queen dismissed her reservations and said, "Why should I wait when I wish this more than either you or he?" They all drew close together. Guenevere leaned toward the knight, who hesitantly imitated her movement though not daring to raise his head. Tall and broad-shouldered, Galehaut arced over them with arms outstretched. In the shelter of this embrace, the queen lifted the young man's chin with her fingertips, bent forward, and gave him a long kiss – which, despite Galehaut's precautions, Blaye did not fail to observe.

After a moment, the queen spoke to the knight: "Dear friend, for all you have done for me I am yours, and that makes me very happy. But now we must take care that no one learn our secret, for the world thinks very well of me, and our love would be a vile and ugly thing if it damaged my reputation." She reflected for the briefest moment, then added, "I ask you, too, wise Galehaut, never to fail my trust, for whatever good or evil comes of this is entirely due to you."

"My lady," said Galehaut, "he could never do anything to harm you, and I have only done what you asked of me. But –" and here he paused, before going on, more softly, "but let me ask you something in return – for now, as I told you yesterday, you can do much more for me than I for you."

Guenevere was inclined to be obliging. "There is nothing I could refuse you."

"Then you will use your power to protect my friendship with Lancelot. Let neither your love nor the interests of this kingdom ever drive us apart."

"Indeed, if I caused you to lose your companion, that would be a poor reward for your generosity. I pledge you my loyal friendship, now and always."

Turning to Lancelot, she said, "And in furtherance of my pledge, I ask you to affirm your commitment to this lord, that you are his forever – except insofar as you are mine."

The knight replied, "The Lord of the Distant Isles has done more for me than anyone has ever done for a friend. We owe him the peace of this kingdom, and I owe him the greatest happiness I have known. I swear always to be loyal to our companionship."

Galehaut thanked him with deep emotion. Whatever this moment meant to the others, to him it contained all the power of an unbreakable covenant. He was grateful for Lancelot's pledge, and glad to have led him where the young man so ardently wished to go. He had not the slightest doubt of the knight's sincerity, though he well knew that passions are not always reined in by solemn promises. Thinking that Lancelot would now be able to enjoy the queen's company alone, he excused himself to confer with his seneschal.

❡ Thus it was that Galehaut brought the queen and Lancelot together and was in turn assured that Lancelot would remain his companion. Night had long fallen by the time Guenevere and the young man rose to leave, but the moon so illuminated the meadow that they could see almost as if it were day. Galehaut rejoined them, and the three walked together, followed by the seneschal and the queen's ladies. When they were opposite Galehaut's tents, Lancelot took leave of the queen and crossed the river with the seneschal. Galehaut escorted Guenevere back to the king, who asked where they had been. "My lord," said Galehaut, "we have been out in the meadow with a few people, as you see." Then they sat down and spoke of many things, Galehaut and the queen feeling much at ease with each other.

A while later, when Guenevere was about to retire for the night, Galehaut told her that he would rejoin his friend and give him what comfort he could. She thanked him for that because "he'll be so glad of your company." Galehaut took leave of the king, and soon he and Lancelot were lying in one bed; they talked all night long of the joy they said was in their hearts.

❡ The queen, sure that she had been very discreet, was standing at a window, rapt in pleasant thoughts, when the chatelaine of Malehaut came up to her and, almost inaudibly, sighed, "Ah, four. . . . Wouldn't that be a welcome number, my lady?"

The queen at first pretended not to hear, but, when the remark was repeated, had no choice. "Why? What do you mean?"

"Perhaps I have already said too much. I don't wish to be presumptuous and offend you."

"On the contrary," said the queen, "I will certainly be displeased if you won't explain."

"I thought of four when I saw the three of you in the

meadow – you, Galehaut, and a certain knight who loves you more than anything else in the world. And no one," she ventured to add, "could be more worthy of your love."

"Oh! Do you know him?"

"Earlier this year he was as much in my power as now he is in yours." And she related how she had offered hospitality to the unknown knight when he had been wounded, and given him the red shield and the black armor in which he had fought so brilliantly. "The day I saw him standing by the battlefield and sent him a message to fight, it was clear to me that you were the one he loved."

"I still don't understand your remark about four."

Blaye explained, "When your knight is away from you, as must happen all too often, at least he can speak of his love to Galehaut. But you will be all alone, with no one to share your secret, unless we make a company of four."

Guenevere was moved by the thought and said, "It's not easy to keep anything from you! But since you have seen so much, and want to share my secret, so you shall. But you will have to share the burden of it as well."

"I will do anything you ask, if I can have your friendship."

"And yours will be so welcome to me that soon I won't be able to live without you! Tell me," the queen went on, "do you know the name of this knight?"

"No, my lady. He always refused to give me his name."

The queen told her that the knight was Lancelot of the Lake, the son of King Ban of Benoic. "Ah," thought Blaye, "the landless prince!" They spoke for a long time, and the queen insisted that Blaye share her bed, which she had been reluctant to do, feeling herself unworthy of such an honor. Before they slept, the queen asked her new friend if she was in love with anyone.

"No," was the reply. "I did love someone once, but it never went beyond my thoughts."

℘ The next morning, they went to the royal pavilion, where Guenevere woke the king, chiding him for lying in bed so long. They left him there with Gawain and other knights, and walked across the meadow to the place where the love pact had been made. The queen relived those moments as she related every detail to Blaye. She went on to praise Galehaut for his wisdom and his discernment. "When I tell him about our friendship, I know he'll be glad for me. In fact, we should leave right now – he may have already returned from his camp."

When she had a moment to speak with Galehaut alone, Guenevere asked him whether there was any maiden or lady to whom he had pledged his love. When he assured her there was not, she said, "I have given my heart as you wished me to, and now I want you to do something similar for me. I have in mind a very noble lady, beautiful and rich, who has become my friend. I would like you to be her friend, too."

Galehaut had a fleeting sense of being played like a piece on a chess board. "I am, of course, at your command, but who is she?"

"Blaye, the Lady of Malehaut. She was watching us last evening in the meadow, and saw everything that happened. She recognized Lancelot. He stayed with her at Malehaut when he had been injured, and it was from there that he went to fight for King Arthur. The red shield and the black armor were her gifts. I think she is worthy of you, and you of her, and that is why I seek to bring you together. When you and my knight must travel far away, you will have each other to share your joys and sorrows, as she and I will do, and all of us will take comfort from having someone to confide in."

"Whatever you desire, my lady," said Galehaut.

The queen turned toward Blaye, who was standing nearby, and asked, "Do you know that I plan to give your heart away?"

"Yes, my lady. It is yours to do with as you will."

The queen took her hand and Galehaut's. "My lord," she said, as decisive in her move as anyone could be, "I give you to this lady to be her knight in true and faithful friendship. And you, lady, I bestow upon this knight to be his true and loyal friend. Do you agree?"

They both said they did, and the queen had them exchange a kiss as a sign of their commitment. Then she said, "I have thought of how the four of us can meet. We will go to our meadow again, but this time invite the king to walk there with us, and many knights and ladies will join us too. When it turns dark, Lancelot can come with the seneschal, and no one will notice him."

That evening, the king walked with the Lady of Malehaut,

84

and Galehaut with the queen, followed by men and women of the court. After a while, Arthur and Guenevere turned aside to talk with King Yder, a paragon of knightly courage and one of Arthur's staunchest allies, who would soon be returning to his own land. Blaye and Galehaut strolled on together, and Blaye began to talk of Lancelot, telling how she had known him before and how greatly she admired him. "He was perfectly courteous," she said, "and grateful for whatever help I could offer, but I always felt in him a great reserve. His beauty astonished me as much as his valor in the field."

Galehaut, touched by this, told how the sight of Lancelot fighting had been a revelation. "My life changed at that moment. I saw what a man could be. Nothing I had cared about in the past was important to me any more. Now I only want what will make him happy."

"The queen has confided in me," said Blaye. "And I'm sure that you and I will find many ways to help them."

Presently they were joined by Lancelot, and they all strolled through the meadow until they came to the grove of apple trees. By now it was quite dark. The queen and one of her ladies met them, and after a while Guenevere took Lancelot by the hand and drew him aside. She sat on the grass with the knight's head in her lap. Silent caresses detained them there for a long time before they returned to the king. Lancelot went back to Galehaut's tents with the seneschal, unobserved. In that way, the lovers were able to be together every night.

There came a time, toward the end of the warm season,

when Sir Gawain had so well recovered from his wounds that he wanted to go home, and hoped to leave within two days. King Arthur had no objection, having delayed his own departure because of his nephew's condition – and also because of his affection for Galehaut.

"Why not, then, invite him to go with you?" Gawain suggested. "His presence in Logres would do you honor. But even if he doesn't come now, I'm sure we'll see him there from time to time."

Galehaut told the king that he too was obliged to return home, where many duties awaited him. "I have only stayed here so long because of you – and I know you have felt the same way."

"I understand, dear friend. Just let me see you again as soon as you can."

Galehaut said he would. That night the four friends met more in sadness than in joy, but they agreed to meet again at the first tournament to be held at Arthur's court. After they parted, the queen bade King Arthur ask the Lady of Malehaut to join the royal household as her companion, and he invited her so warmly that she could only accept.

BOOK SIX + LANCELOT AND GALEHAUT

IT TOOK SEVERAL DAYS FOR GALEHAUT and Lancelot to reach the land called Sorelais, between Wales and the Distant Isles, and far from Arthur's kingdom. Conquered from the King of Northumberland, it was the favorite of Galehaut's possessions, with forests full of game, broad rivers, and rich farmlands. There were beautiful fortified towns and fine castles. Surrounding Sorelais, in the direction of Logres, was a great river called the Severn; the rest of the country was bordered by the sea. The Severn was swift-flowing, wide, and very deep. It could be crossed only at two points where there were long, narrow causeways, each guarded by a tower where a knight and ten men-at-arms kept watch. A knight wanting to cross was obliged to fight them, and if he lost, he was not merely turned back, but was entirely at their mercy. Men thought it an honor to be chosen for this post, which each defender held for a year and for which he was well paid. In this way, Sorelais was protected from intruders. Anyone brave and skilled enough to win his way across the river would be a welcome guest.

Galehaut kept his return to Sorelais as quiet as he could, attending to his duties as overlord but making no great display of his presence; and, except for the First Defeated King and the King of the Hundred Knights, no one knew who his companion was. There was fine hunting in Sorelais, which

Galehaut always enjoyed, but Lancelot was given over to sadness, unable to think of anything but the queen. It pained Galehaut to witness his companion's distress and to realize how little he could do to help him. The only comfort was the hope that news of a tournament would come before long.

Within a month of their arrival, the Lady of the Lake sent Lancelot's cousin Lionel to serve as his squire until he was of age to become a knight. Lancelot was overjoyed to see him again, and it was easy to obey the Lady's command that he hold Lionel as dear as herself. His unhappiness about the queen subsided, and Galehaut was equally delighted to welcome the handsome youth. If his affection alone could not bring cheer to Lancelot, he was satisfied to see his efforts reinforced by the presence of the newcomer. Lionel and his younger brother Bors were the sons of King Bors, King Ban's brother, and his wife Evaine. On the death of their father, they had been captured and imprisoned by King Claudas but then magically rescued by the Lady of the Lake, who gave them the semblance of two fine greyhounds and thus brought them in disguise to the kingdom under the lake. There she had raised them with Lancelot. So Lionel now brought to Sorelais a reminder of the happiness they had shared in that charmed domain.

℄ King Arthur, meanwhile, had been traveling through his lands, celebrating his return from the encounter with Galehaut with showers of largesse and splendid festivities for the delight of his people. Queen Guenevere and the Lady of Malehaut accompanied him, comforting each other, in endless private conversations, for the absence of those they loved. One afternoon, a squire announced to the queen that a maiden had come to see her with a message from the Lady of the Lake. Guenevere received her with pleasure, and the maiden presented a gift, a beautifully painted shield. On it were portrayed a noble woman of extraordinary beauty and a magnificent knight, fully armored except that he wore no helmet. They would have been joined in an embrace, had it not been for a crack that ran the length of the shield, so wide that a hand could easily pass through it. Only the strong cross-piece of the boss kept the two halves together.

The queen marveled at this, and asked how the shield, which appeared so new, had come to be cracked, and who were the knight and lady it portrayed. The maiden replied that the knight, who surpassed all others in valor, had served the lady with absolute devotion, performing for her sake deeds that were the wonder of the world. So far he had received from her only a partial expression of love, but when his reward was complete, the shield would be made whole. "My wise and beautiful mistress has charged me to say that she is the person closest to you in the world, that she knows your very thoughts, for she loves the same knight you do."

The queen detained her visitor for a while, wanting to do her honor, grateful for the gift and for its meaning. She had no doubt who the knight must be.

After visiting Camelot and Carleon, the king went to Carduel, his favorite city, where for two weeks he held court, inviting all who would appeal for justice to come before him. The king and his advisors heard every case with wisdom and generosity, all of them eager to do what was right and just.

When the audiences were over, the queen and Blaye were going to suggest a date for a tournament, but the king suddenly turned so melancholy that no entertainments could be envisioned. At length, his barons persuaded him to say what was preoccupying him. His court was dishonored, he told them, because the Red Knight had never been found, despite the fact that forty knights, led by Gawain, had spent almost a year searching for him. He himself was shamed – not only they – by the failure of their mission, and "is the very honor of the realm not thereby blemished?" Now, however, with his nephew's health almost completely restored, the search could be resumed.

Gawain said to the king, in a voice loud enough to be heard throughout the hall, "You are right, my lord, and what you say is true. It would be shameful if I stayed here any longer! I swear by almighty God that you will not see me again before I have either found the Red Knight or learned what became of him."

The knights of his own household, and fourteen others who had joined the earlier quest, resolved to arm themselves and set out anew.

But Arthur was jolted by their alacrity. After all, recent events had effaced the importance of that quest. Had the success of the Red Knight not proved a passing moment on the way toward the extraordinary achievement of the Black Knight? In truth, Arthur could ill afford to have a score of his finest knights out wandering, when the court required their protective presence. He wished he could take back his words. He went to tell the queen what had happened, imploring her to prevent Gawain from leaving, since nothing he himself could say was likely to change matters.

In her nephew's chambers, the queen found Gawain already armed and about to depart. If she thought it would be easy to dissuade him, she was wrong. She argued that many knights who would be eager to accompany him were away from court and that the king bitterly regretted having spoken as he did: indeed Arthur was almost beside himself with grief. Gawain replied that he would rather die than act against his honor, and that nothing whatsoever could change his mind. "If I should die on this quest, at least I will not be shamed. I will never return to the king's presence, until I have found the Red Knight, although," he added plaintively, "I have no idea where to look for him."

Guenevere saw that dissuasion would not prevail. She decided to spare her nephew needless effort by offering him a confidence. "I will tell you how to find the Red Knight, if you promise to keep it secret from everyone."

Gawain did not hesitate. "I swear it."

"He will be with Galehaut, if he is anywhere."

No announcement could have been more exhilarating.

Gawain rushed to inform the knights who had intended to share his quest that he would proceed alone. Refusing to waste time listening to their protests, he took a hasty leave of the court and galloped away. The king was sure that he would never see him again.

℄ Lionel's presence in Sorelais had at first distracted Lancelot from his unhappiness, but it was not long before his separation from the queen began once again to depress his spirits. As the weeks and months went by, he gradually lost all interest in his surroundings, until he was scarcely able to eat, drink, or sleep. He told Galehaut that he was dying.

"Dearest friend," said Galehaut, "would you feel better if you could see the queen?"

"Of course I would."

"Then I'll find a way to make that happen."

"But I know that she would send for us if it were possible, and I'd rather die than cause her any pain."

"I'm sure it would do no harm to have Lionel take her a message."

"As you think best."

Galehaut, meeting with Lionel privately, told him he was to travel to Arthur's court with a message for the queen, and for her alone. He was to ask for the Lady of Malehaut, on behalf of the Lord of the Distant Isles. He would be carrying a ring that the lady would be sure to recognize as Galehaut's. When she saw it, Lionel's request for an interview with the queen would certainly be granted. Galehaut told him how things were between Lancelot and Guenevere. "When you see that peerless woman, take care to show yourself worthy of such an honor. If she asks who you are, tell her that your father was Bors of Gaunes, and that Lancelot of the Lake is your first cousin. If she asks about her friend, say that he cannot fare well deprived of her presence. Tell her we hope she will soon find a way for him to see her because our – yes, our – suffering is more than we can bear."

Lionel said he would not fail to deliver the message faithfully, not omitting a word.

"Go then," said Galehaut, "and let no one know whom you serve or where you are going. It could cost us our lives, and you your honor."

"I would let my eyes be torn out before I'd betray you!" And then he was on his way.

But Lionel was still very young, and only a squire. One day as he rode through Logres, he saw a crowd of people running toward an enclosed field just outside the walls of Cambenic, a ducal city. Wondering what was happening, he went closer and learned that a judicial combat was in progress: an unknown knight was fighting the duke's seneschal, who had wrongly accused an elderly man of treason. Lionel had never seen such a duel. He pushed his way through so eagerly that his horse jostled some knights who were watching the combat. One of these shouted at him to go back, but Lionel was so absorbed he did not hear him. The knight grasped Lionel's horse by the reins, turned him around sharply, and raised a cudgel. Lionel, who had nearly fallen off, drew his sword, but a young woman cried out for him to stop: a squire must never attack a knight. The youth put his sword away, "but a knight," he said, "should never conduct himself shamefully! I don't care about seeing your battle – my master would have defeated both of these men without turning a hair!"

The knight, laughing, asked who his master was.

"You're better off not knowing! Not for all the lands of Galehaut would you want to see him up close!"

He regretted his words too late. Ashamed and confused, Lionel left the combat and hurried out of town into the forest. The knight fighting for the defense, however, had overheard the angry exchange. Anxious to question the squire, he redoubled the ferocity of his attack, and his treacherous opponent, who had thought himself close to winning, was soon defeated. The accusation of treason was thus disproved. The defendant, saved from death, had scarcely begun to express his gratitude when his champion galloped away into the forest. At a turn in the path, his horse nearly collided with the young man, now on foot. Reining in his mount, the knight shouted, "What are you doing here? What happened to your horse?"

Lionel, however, was learning to be cautious. "First tell me, on your honor as a knight, who you are."

"I am Gawain, King Arthur's nephew." Before Lionel could

respond, he went on, "I heard you mention Galehaut. I want you to know that the Lord of the Distant Isles is very dear to me. That's why, if anyone has wronged you, I swear you'll be avenged!"

Lionel was visibly relieved. "Then I'll tell you what happened," he said. "I had scarcely left the battle and ridden into the forest when a knight, on foot, ran toward me and seized my horse. I didn't try to fight him because he was fully armed, and because I have no right to attack a knight, but now I think I should have died trying."

"Which way did he go?"

"My horse's tracks are just over there, my lord. He's a roan with a white blaze."

"Then follow me as best you can. I'll either get your horse back for you or give you my own!"

"How can I thank you, my lord!"

Sir Gawain galloped through the forest into a valley where he saw two knights fighting on foot, their horses, one of which was Lionel's, tied to a tree. "Stop, my lords! Don't make another move before you tell me which of you rode this horse!"

"I did," said one of the knights; "what's that to you?"

"It's something to me when a knight takes a horse from a harmless squire! You are to declare yourself his prisoner as reparation!"

"Brave words, my friend! Let's see how you back them up!"

"Be careful!" said his opponent, clearly pleased with this

turn of events. "That's the best knight you've ever seen! He has just defeated the duke's seneschal!"

"Then I certainly won't try to fight him! My lord," he went on, seeking to placate the newcomer, "do with me as you will. It was because I really needed a mount that I took the squire's horse. Here is my sword. I ask only that you let me know your name."

"I have never concealed my name from anyone who asked. I am King Arthur's nephew, Gawain."

The other knight said, "Noble as you are, I won't complain that you deprived me of my battle! It is an honor."

"What was your quarrel about?" asked Gawain.

"He said he was a better fighter than I, and I wanted to prove him wrong. I won the first joust, and caught his horse who was running away. Then he found your squire in the forest."

Gawain, satisfied, brought the exchange to a close with a quick judgment. "If your cause was as little as that, you would do better to stay friends."

Then the three of them rode back to meet Lionel. Gawain said, "Dear brother, here is the knight who stole your horse. Ask him whatever you wish as reparation."

"Thank you, my lord! Now I know for certain that you are Sir Gawain!"

The guilty knight returned Lionel's horse; then he knelt before him and asked for mercy. The squire had him rise. When Gawain repeated that he could take whatever retribution he thought best, the boy said, "My lord, I ask nothing more of him, except that he give his word as a knight never again to attack a man not in full armor, and that he will do his best to help anyone so attacked." Sir Gawain took the man's oath. Then he gave the two knights leave to go, and they rode away.

⁋ As soon as they were alone, Gawain asked Lionel to give him news of Galehaut. "My lord, I am not in his service."

"But you do know where he is."

Lionel felt caught between loyalty to Galehaut and gratitude to Gawain. He paused, then said slowly and distinctly, "If he were in Sorelais, my lord, you would find it hard to reach him. You would have to fight your way in."

Gawain realized that he would learn nothing more but had learned enough. He commended the squire to God, and they took leave of each other. Gawain lost no time in starting out for Sorelais, and Lionel went his way toward King Arthur's court.

⁋ He found the king in the capital city of his realm, and there the Lady of Malehaut and the queen herself welcomed him warmly even before they learned who he was. They were glad to have news of Sir Gawain, and the youth related the knight's successful fight with the Duke of Cambenic's seneschal. "And my horse had been stolen, and he got it back for me. He rode with me for a while, asking where I was going, but I didn't tell him." Lionel gave them the message from Lancelot and Galehaut, exactly as he had been told to, and the two ladies immediately began trying to think of a way to see them. Now that they had good news of Gawain, it might be possible to introduce the idea of a tournament.

However, while the ladies were discussing how best to proceed, messengers arrived with news of war in Scotland. A plan to play at war was thus suddenly displaced by the reality of war! Saxon and Irish invaders were ravaging the land and massacring large numbers of people. Already they held much of the country, and were threatening an important castle near Arestel.

King Arthur, dismayed by the news, sent urgent messages to his vassals, directing them to present themselves at Carduel with all the forces they could muster. They were to be there within two weeks. Lionel, on the queen's order, set out for Sorelais. He was to inform Lancelot and Galehaut of the invasion, and tell them where to meet the king in Scotland. They were to travel in disguise. She sent Lancelot a red silk pennon for his helmet, so that she could recognize him in his armor, and also a ring from her finger as a token of her love. After the boy had left, King Arthur asked Guenevere whether he should seek to have Galehaut join him. She seemed to reflect for a moment, then suggested that he wait until he knew how much help he would really need, since "you don't want him to think you are afraid."

℧ Both Gawain and Lionel were riding, separately, toward Sorelais, the one knowing the way, but the other well in the lead. Gawain had the help of a hermit who was able to give useful directions. The hermit explained that Galehaut, intent on protecting the inhabitants of Sorelais from those who might want to rob or otherwise injure them, had established guard posts at the only two points of entry. Those who crossed the bridges would be challenged by a skilled knight, backed by men-at-arms. The Lord of the Distant Isles believed that anyone who defeated such a defender would have proven worthy of confidence and so allowed to pass. Thus it was not too long before Sir Gawain came to the first causeway over the Severn. It was massive, high, and extremely long and dangerous. In the distance he could see the imposing tower of the castle guarding the entry to Sorelais. A squire had accompanied him, riding a fine palfrey and leading Gawain's warhorse. Gawain said the warhorse would be all he would need from now on. He made a gift of the palfrey to the squire, and told him that he was free to go. The young man, out of gratitude, waited to see what would happen on the causeway, climbing a nearby hill to have a better view.

Down below, a well-armed knight rode out to meet Gawain and said that if he planned to enter the country, he would have to fight him first.

"I certainly plan to enter," answered Gawain.

"And, should you defeat me, you will have to deal with my ten men-at-arms." These were already arriving, armed with axes as well as swords.

"I want simply to be sure that only these ten will be involved."

"They will be quite enough! But if you should defeat us, custom demands that you guard the causeway until a replacement arrives."

Gawain accepted the conditions, more concerned about the delay than the odds. The ten men-at-arms withdrew and stood close together, as Gawain rode back along the causeway to where he could turn and gallop at full speed toward the knight who came rushing toward him. In the shock of their encounter, Gawain's lance shattered his opponent's shield. Then, with his lance still unbroken, he whirled around and struck the knight full in the center of his chest, though the weapon did not penetrate far past the chain-mail hauberk. The knight fell unconscious to the ground, and Gawain, not wanting to dismount for fear of losing his horse, drew his sword, approached the knight, who was just reviving, and told him he would die unless he surrendered. The sight of blood streaming over his body made him fear that he would die without confession, so, asking Gawain for mercy, he declared himself vanquished. But even as he was handing over his sword, the ten men-at-arms, lowborn knaves awkward even in light armor, rushed forward to attack, striking heavy blows with their axes and swords. In no time they had killed Gawain's horse, but they could not injure the knight himself.

At that point, the squire, who had been watching all the

while, spurred his horse and galloped out onto the causeway, shouting, "Bastards! Every one of you will hang if you kill Sir Gawain! He's the greatest knight in the world and King Arthur's nephew!"

With that he struck one of them so hard he fell down dead. The others took flight, some toward the tower, some to the river bank. There was a tense silence. The squire dismounted and secured the wounded knight's charger for his lord. One of the men who had fled into the tower came out with the keys of the castle, which he presented to Gawain saying, "Welcome, sir! You have nothing to fear from us!" The wounded knight was comforted to know who had defeated him, and Gawain accompanied him back to the castle, after saying farewell to the squire.

They inscribed Gawain's name on a stone slab commemorating those who had crossed the causeway. There were only five names, the first of them, dating from long before, King Arthur's. The vanquished were also recorded, and Elinant, just defeated by Gawain, was one of the best knights in Galehaut's kingdom.

A squire had already left the causeway, carrying word to Galehaut that an unknown knight had defeated Elinant and the men-at-arms. Galehaut declared he was eager to meet a warrior so valiant, but Lancelot was determined to fight him. He had nothing to do but wait for Lionel to return, and a challenging battle would be a most welcome relief from frustration. Hunting was no substitute for jousting! "We might as well be in prison here! We are wasting our time and our youth, doing nothing worthy of knights."

Galehaut smiled at this, but resolved to prevent any such confrontation. That evening one of his knights, Elias of Ragres, asked if he could have the command of the causeway, and Galehaut, knowing his valor, gave permission.

Thus Gawain was relieved of his obligation. He ordered Elinant to present himself to King Arthur, and to inform the king and queen that he would return as soon as he could. Then he started into the interior of Sorelais. Elinant too set out immediately, although it was painful for him to travel. Arthur and Guenevere welcomed him, very glad to have news of Gawain, but the king was troubled to learn that his nephew had not yet accomplished his quest. Aided by neither Gawain nor the Red Knight, it was only with great reluctance that he was going to war in Scotland. The queen made sure that Elinant's wounds were treated skillfully, and when he was well enough, he joined King Arthur's household.

℘ Galehaut had persuaded Lancelot to accompany him to an island in the middle of the Severn, where he had a fine castle with a high stone tower. The place was connected to the mainland by a drawbridge but was otherwise so isolated that it was called Lost Island. Though the surroundings were beautiful, Lancelot, endlessly longing to see the queen, took no pleasure in them. He spent his time in the tower, brooding and watching the river day after day, with nothing to relieve the monotony or his sadness – until, one morning, not long after the news of the causeway, he noticed a knight on the opposite bank! Sure that this must be the one who had crossed the Severn, he could not contain his excitement. He rushed down the stairs to tell Galehaut, who quickly dispatched a servant to find out what the stranger wanted. "But be sure," he warned, "that you don't tell him I am here!"

After his victory at the entry to Sorelais, Gawain had wandered through the countryside, asking people everywhere for news of their lord Galehaut. One day he had encountered a girl on horseback who said she would help him, "if you will grant me a boon when I ask it of you." When he had promised her that he would, she led him to the top of a high hill and pointed to Lost Island. "My lord is there, but wants to see no one."

Gawain, now so close to his goal, refused to accept this discouraging statement. He was sure that no reclusiveness would stop Galehaut from receiving Gawain himself, and with pleasure. He had, though, to conceal his identity for a while if he was to succeed as he wished with the Red Knight, and succeed in more than one way.

Ever since he had witnessed the Red Knight's astonishing feats on the battlefield, Gawain had harbored a keen, unspoken ambition to match his own prowess against the strength and combat skill of the stranger. There had been no earlier opportunity, but now Gawain had recovered from his last injuries and was filled with energy. How better to express his admiration for the Red Knight than to face him in a duel?

But the Red Knight, having fought in defense of King Arthur, might be unwilling to oppose the king's nephew. No, thought Sir Gawain, he had to keep his name a secret. The combat had to take place, moreover, for another, more practical reason. However supportive of the king the unknown knight had been, he had, in the end, chosen to remain unidentified and to have nothing further to do with Arthur's court. Gawain, to achieve his quest, had not only to find the Red Knight but also to lead him back to the king. This might be possible only if the knight were defeated in battle. So Gawain felt fully justified in provoking an armed encounter.

Gawain told the servant that he intended to stay where he was, ready to fight anyone who attempted to drive him away. "But it seems to me very strange that two knights would hide from one!"

Galehaut, informed, thought this excessively haughty and, to teach the knight a lesson, sent one of his best fighters to challenge him. The drawbridge was let down, and Gawain saw a horseman galloping toward him. "Surrender to me or fight!"

"If it's up to you to guard the place, there's no need for me to surrender!" With that taunt, Gawain rode out onto the bridge and charged. An instant later, the knight was catapulted backwards off his horse, hitting the ground with a thud. Gawain quickly dismounted, drew his sword, pulled the helmet off his opponent's head, and demanded that he yield.

There was no argument. Gawain secured his prisoner, while Galehaut, watching from the castle, admired his prowess. He called for his armor. But Lancelot insisted that he would be the one to challenge the stranger, and Galehaut reluctantly agreed.

℄ Although he was now wearing different armor, Gawain recognized the Red Knight from the way he sat his horse. The queen had been right: he was now facing the man he had long been seeking. But in the instant his opponent came charging toward him, he remembered too the greatest knight he had ever seen, a man in black armor against whom no one could stand. Gawain and Lancelot came together with such tremendous force that both fell to the ground with their horses on top of them. They quickly disengaged themselves and jumped up, swords in hand. The duel went on for a long time. After noon Gawain's strength diminished, as it always did at that time; Lancelot began to prevail. Gawain's shield was in tatters, and there were gaping holes in his coat of mail. He felt he was close to death. But Lancelot too had suffered serious wounds. Gawain succeeded in surmounting his weakness; indeed, his strength gradually doubled. Now Galehaut feared for his friend. Gawain's fighting was brilliant, but just when it seemed that Lancelot was facing defeat and death, Lionel arrived at the drawbridge and watched, aghast, the two friends who had turned into foes.

Just then, Lancelot sprang at Gawain with new ferocity and

power. In a moment, he had the advantage. Lionel cried out to him, "Stop! By the order of the queen!" Lancelot instantly drew back, and Lionel shouted that he was fighting Sir Gawain. The two adversaries stood immobilized.

Sick with grief and shame, Lancelot threw down his sword, and gasped, "What have I done?" He ran to his horse, but Gawain jumped up behind him and held him so that they rode through the gates of the castle together. Galehaut was there when they dismounted. He saw that Lancelot was in such distress he could not speak, and asked Gawain to wait for a few moments until he recovered. While servants attended to the visitor, Galehaut led Lancelot into a chamber, where he tried to find out what had happened to grieve him so. Finally Lancelot blurted out that he had lost the queen's love forever by injuring her nephew. Galehaut helped Lancelot take off his armor and wash his face. Then he said, "I'll bring Gawain to you, and you can ask his forgiveness. Tell him you're ready to do whatever he wishes."

Galehaut returned to Gawain. "Tell me, my lord," he said, "do you know who it is you were fighting?"

"I know that it was the Red Knight, who won the field when you first brought your army against us."

"... and who because of you is mortified with shame and grief!"

When they entered the room, Galehaut said, "Here is my lord Gawain."

Lancelot fell to his knees before him and asked his forgiveness. Gawain was astonished to recognize the young man whose beauty had touched everyone when he had first come to court with the Lady of the Lake. He raised him to his feet and put his arms around him, saying, "King Arthur charged me to find the Red Knight, but I have also found the one who rescued me from hopeless captivity."

"Can you forgive me, my lord, for the harm I have done today? Truly, I did not know who you were."

"You have done a hundred times more for me than I for you!" And as he uttered those words, Gawain saw, in a flash of recognition, the Black Knight leaving the field with Galehaut's hand on his shoulder. "And not just for me! Isn't it thanks to you that my uncle still rules his kingdom? that the Lord of the Distant Isles sacrificed his honor and surrendered? Truly, you owe me nothing. But out of friendship, tell me – I would be grateful to know – tell me, at last, who you are."

The young man said, "I am Lancelot of the Lake. My father was King Ban of Benoic."

They embraced, elated and moved by all that they now understood. But both had serious wounds, and Galehaut's doctors, attending to their treatment, insisted they rest. Nevertheless, all that afternoon and far into the night, they talked. Now Galehaut learned how Lancelot had conquered Dolorous Guard, "and then brought me the help I sorely needed when I was being held by Brandis," added Gawain.

"My lord, I have never forgotten how kind you were to me when I wasn't yet a knight."

Then Gawain asked how it was that the Lady of the Lake had brought King Ban's son to Arthur, and Lancelot told more than he had yet confided even to Galehaut. He spoke of those years when he knew nothing about his father, and believed that Viviane was his mother. A time would come for him to avenge his father's death and reclaim his birthright.

℘ They spent several more days on the island, delighted to be with one another. Lionel spoke privately to Galehaut, giving him the queen's message. Galehaut kept it to himself for a while, knowing that, the moment they heard about the invasion, and regardless of their condition, the two knights would insist on starting out. When their strength was somewhat restored, he gave them the news and the queen's instructions. They were all to go to Scotland in disguise, but wearing the tokens Guenevere would recognize. She herself would inform them how they best could help the king. Galehaut asked the King of the Hundred Knights and the First Defeated King to go with them, along with a number of his household knights and squires. Lionel was included, as a reward for having carried out his missions with courage and good sense. Before setting out, they waited only long enough for a pack train to be loaded with their equipment.

They had not ridden very far when they encountered the girl who had helped Gawain find Lost Island. When they asked her if she had heard news of King Arthur, she told them that indeed she had – reliable news – but did not intend to give it away without a promise from them. They must agree to accompany her whenever she required it, up to a league's distance away.

"We will do as you ask," said Lancelot, and Galehaut also gave his word.

"The king is already at Arestel. You will find him besieging the fortress they call Saxon Rock."

They commended her to God, and she returned their farewell. Then, leaving the pack train to follow them more slowly, the knights galloped northward.

D AYS OF HARD RIDING WENT BY
before they arrived at Arestel and learned that
the king was indeed encamped before Saxon
Rock, a fortress so strong that only famine could
overcome it. It had been secretly built by the treacherous
Vortigern, the king who had let Saxons into Britain many
years before. Four leagues lay between the town of Arestel
and the fortress, and everything in the area had been razed to
the ground except for one manor house, very close to Saxon
Rock. There lived the enchantress Gamille, a Saxon by birth,
and extremely beautiful. She had thoroughly bewitched King
Arthur, who went every day to plead for her favor, without
ever receiving the slightest encouragement. He could think
of nothing but her.

Saxon and Irish knights had come out onto the battlefield
in great numbers that day, hoping to inflict enough losses on
the Britons to make them withdraw. As the sound of fighting
grew louder, Gawain told Galehaut that because of his oath
he could not enter the king's presence unless to reveal the successful accomplishment of his quest for the Red Knight. Galehaut asked him to wait until the end of the siege, "and then
Lancelot will surely go with you." Gawain agreed.

The queen and Blaye of Malehaut were in the tower of
a house where they were lodging. Watching the armed men

ride by, they recognized Lancelot and Galehaut by the red pennon on Lancelot's helmet. It was not long before Lancelot received a message from the queen, telling him that she would be pleased to have the fighting, should he be in it, take place where she could see it from her tower.

The king himself was fighting that day, surpassing himself in valor; he was eager to impress Gamille. There were not many men with him as he galloped toward a large company of Saxon warriors. Lancelot, heeding the queen's command, suggested that the forces brought from Sorelais ride up behind the Saxons as if to reinforce them. Gawain hesitated to appear to attack his lord and uncle, but Lancelot assured him that the king would benefit in the end. At the sight of so many un-known warriors approaching, Arthur's knights began to retreat toward the river near their camp. The Saxons, frantic to have their victory, followed them over the ford, not far from the queen's observation post.

Suddenly there was a shout of "Let's get them!" from Lance-lot, and Arthur, recognizing allies, was able to turn his knights back toward the enemy. The Saxons were surrounded. Lance-lot, Galehaut, and Gawain rode side by side at the entrance to the ford, cutting down any who hoped to escape that way. The bodies were piled so high they made a dam in the river, and the place was known thereafter as the Red Ford. Mean-while, attacking the enemy horde from the other side, King Arthur's men captured Aramont, the Saxon king's brother; and many others were made prisoners or left for dead. Lancelot had taken so many blows that his helmet was dented and cracked. The queen, frightened for him, sent a splendid new one – indeed, a helmet belonging to the king – but with a message ordering him to stop the slaughter and let the remaining Saxons escape.

They hurled themselves across the ford, but King Arthur's men and Lancelot's were soon upon them again, making them pay dearly for any distance they gained on their flight back to the fortress. But the Saxons and their Irish allies were skilled and courageous fighters. Had it not been for Lancelot, Arthur would have fared very badly in this encounter. Two of the king's horses were killed under him, and the third fell and broke its neck. His own men were too involved in their chase to notice, and it was Lancelot who remounted the king each time.

It was almost dark when the surviving Saxons regained their fortress. Gawain made himself known to a few of the knights of his household who had been on the field, while Galehaut and Lancelot rode off toward the queen's tower. She and Blaye came down to greet them. When she saw Lancelot with blood streaking his left shoulder, Guenevere feared for his life, but he said he was scarcely hurt, and "besides, I have no fear of death, as long as you wish me well." She took him in her arms, chain mail and all, and promised that she would heal him before morning. "You must leave me now," she whispered, "but send Lionel to me later."

The two knights rode to where their tents had been set up between Arthur's army and Arestel, in a peaceful site on the edge of a woodland. It was surrounded by a tall palisade, and closed with a gate; someone from Arestel had planted a garden there. Galehaut's pavilion was magnificent, with ample room for both him and his companion, and also for the ten squires he had with him. The knights would ride out from there to join the fighting, and return only after dark so they would not be recognized.

C When King Arthur left the battlefield, he rode to Gamille's manor, accompanied by only one discreet squire. This evening, for the first time, the lady had sent word that he might visit her there. The king was overjoyed when she came to the gate to welcome him. "My lord, you are the most valiant man of our times, and you have allowed me to believe that you love me above all other women. Now I will put your courage to a test."

More tempted by this enchantress than he had ever been before, Arthur did not hesitate, but said, "There is nothing I would not do for you."

"That remains to be seen. I want you to sleep with me tonight – not here, but in the fortress of Saxon Rock itself."

Arthur was no less direct in his response. "If you promise me the pleasure a knight may hope to have with a lady."

Assured that all his desires would be fulfilled, he said he would come to her as soon as he had seen to his knights and dined with them.

She replied, "My messenger will be waiting for you just beyond your camp."

His knights had never seen their sovereign so exuberant. He sent a message to the queen, saying he would not be with her that night, and inviting her to rejoice in the success of the day's fighting. Guenevere was not particularly sorry to have this news. When Lionel came to her lodgings that evening, she sent him back to tell Lancelot that she would meet him in a garden inside the walls, on the far side of the tower, later that night. The gate would be unlocked. But he was to come on horseback, fully armed.

℘ As soon as the knights in the king's tent were asleep, Arthur and his nephew Guerrehet, who was in his confidence, rose very quietly and armed themselves. Gamille's guide was waiting for them, and they rode together to the fortress, full of expectation. The lady welcomed them warmly, while squires helped them remove their armor. A lovely maiden led Guerrehet to another room.

Alone now with Gamille, Arthur was too enthralled to realize how vulnerable he was. She was, after all, allied with his enemies, and he was even meeting her in the fortress he had resolved to conquer. But her allure was too potent to resist, and her readiness to comply with his desire swept away all caution. She guided him toward a splendid bed whose soft fur covers merged with the smoothness of her flesh to work an inescapable magic.

King Arthur was so caught up in his pleasure that he failed to hear the heavy footsteps and the clink of armor just outside the door, and was astonished when armed knights burst in, more than forty of them, swords in hand. The king jumped up and reached for his weapon, but he was unclothed, and could not defend himself. Torches were suddenly blazing in the chamber, and Arthur realized that all he could do was surrender. Guerrehet was taken in the same way. They were given their clothes and thrust into a room whose strong walls and single iron door made escape impossible.

℄ Lancelot and Galehaut waited until everyone else was fast asleep, then rose, and, with Galehaut's help, Lancelot armed himself. Galehaut bade him goodbye outside their pavilion and stood for a long moment watching wistfully as Lancelot rode away.

At the tower, the young knight found the garden door unlocked as promised. There were no guards on this side because deep water and marshlands protected the walls. He closed and locked the gate behind him and rode in. The queen was waiting. The horse was stabled, the visitor disarmed, and the couple went to a private chamber in the part of the tower which housed only the queen and her ladies.

For Lancelot and Guenevere, the night was both a culmination and a new beginning, a moment snatched from battle and from a marriage fixed in loyalty if not fidelity. Galehaut's sacrifice had led to this night's union, the more easily because of Arthur's indifference. As warfare and subterfuge trapped the king, Guenevere could grant her lover the unreserved fulfillment he had longed for. He had dedicated his valor to her, had fought to win renown the better to deserve her love, had wielded his powerful sword ever aware that, having come from her, it demanded the utmost bravery of its possessor. One woman had foreseen what his destiny would be, and had nurtured in him the gifts necessary to achieve it; another was at last acknowledging his merit.

From their first, life-transforming, kiss, the queen was now allowing them to progress to the full realization of their love; a yearning of which they had often heard the poets sing was now producing the wondrous union that the singers could only imagine. The night's rich darkness brought them perfect joy.

Toward midnight, the queen arose, remembering the mysterious shield sent by the Lady of the Lake, the shield that would not be whole until the world's most valiant knight and his peerless lady came together to celebrate the perfection of their love. Now, in the darkness, Guenevere ran her hands over the heavy tooled leather. The crack was gone. The shield was flawless.

℄ The next morning, Lancelot, too, was filled with wonder, gazing at the restored shield. What it might portend was soon put into words as Guenevere softly began to urge her lover to give his allegiance to the Round Table and remain at the royal court. She, who at first had been hardly more than amused by his infatuation, could not now bear the thought that he might

leave with Galehaut. She knew that Lancelot had found in this great king a companion of extraordinary generosity, a potent ally in any attempt he might make to reconquer the land which was his birthright. In Sorelais, his interests would be more than amply served. But she loved him too much to sacrifice his presence for his welfare, and believed that Lancelot would feel the same way. He responded only by telling her that he would return the next night.

⟨ Lancelot was no sooner back at Galehaut's pavilion than the two companions heard great roars resounding from Saxon Rock, and it was not long before they grasped that these were sounds of rejoicing. The explanation was soon apparent. King Arthur's shield, along with Guerrehet's, hung from the parapet! It could only mean the two men had been taken captive, and it was a painful disgrace. The Britons were overwhelmed with grief to find themselves bereft of their powerful leader. Sir Gawain was near despair, but Lancelot vowed, "We'll rescue him or be taken prisoners ourselves." The queen, too, had just learned the news and sent word to Lancelot and Galehaut to come to her tower. She was anxious for their help – but they had already disappeared.

Out of nowhere, it seemed, the girl who had helped Gawain find Galehaut, the same girl who had told them that the king was at Arestel, suddenly burst into their tent to remind them of their debt: they were to grant her the first boon she asked, and the moment had come.

"You have chosen a bad time," said Galehaut. "King Arthur has been captured by the Saxons – we can think of nothing else!"

"That's exactly why I have come! They're going to take him away and hide him in Ireland! You can rescue him if you come with me right now! The king has no idea what they have planned."

Fully armed, Lancelot, Galehaut, and Gawain leapt onto their horses. Soon they were following their guide through a long underground gallery beneath Saxon Rock. They could scarcely see one another in the darkness. King Arthur and Guerrehet, she said, would be brought through that passageway. Gawain and Galehaut were each to guard an exit that she showed them, quite far from each other, while Lancelot was to stay where he was and wait for her signal.

Lancelot stood there for a long time, in utter silence, until suddenly he was startled by the young woman's cries for help. "Here he is!" she shouted. As Lancelot rushed toward the sound, someone lighted a torch and Lancelot could see two knights, one in the king's armor, one in Guerrehet's, defending themselves against more than twenty Saxons. Sword in hand, he ran to the king's side, but the pair he intended to rescue turned on him instead and threw him to the ground. Others seized his sword and shield, and slashed the laces of his helmet. They threatened to cut off his head unless he surrendered. That he refused to do, not caring, in his rage, whether he lived or died. Overwhelmed by their numbers, he could not prevent them from carrying him, still struggling, to a cell, where they locked him in.

Galehaut saw a knight in Lancelot's armor who seemed to be fighting against great odds. Deceived just like his friend, he was soon captured. Gawain suffered the same fate, although he too defended himself heroically. Then, having given their word to their assailants to renounce any attempts to escape, they were left in a cell together, unbound. Lancelot, however, refused to yield, although they threatened to keep him chained and in prison forever. He said he had no desire except for death.

℮ Guenevere was also ready to die when, after a sleepless night, she saw the three newly captured shields displayed at Saxon Rock. Sir Yvain came to try to bring her comfort, and she fell weeping at his feet, imploring him to do his best for her honor and the king's. He raised her up with tears in his own eyes, for never was a lady so much loved by her lord's knights as was this queen.

Yvain, that day, took King Arthur's place in the battle; Sir Kay, as always, carried the royal banner. The Saxons and their Irish allies were sure that Arthur's army would be demoralized without the king and the great knights they had captured, but as soon as the battalions began to sweep across the field, they saw they were mistaken. Of the many valiant deeds performed by the Britons, none surpassed the accomplishments of King Yder, his white and crimson banner flying above him, as his matchless horse carried him through the thick of the Saxon hordes. Horse and man were red with their enemies' blood and their own. Yder would be crippled and in pain for the rest of his life, but, as knights on both sides acclaimed him, he prayed that God would allow him to go on fighting until victory was won. After that, he would gladly die, for he knew he would never again have a day so full of glory.

As the Saxons began to flee, Arthur's troops cut them down in great numbers. King Yder's horse was still galloping freely, but as it leapt over a Saxon on the ground, the man reached up with his sword and slashed its belly open. Even with that mortal wound, the superb charger rushed on toward Saxon Rock until, at last, it could do no more. Its rider fell unconscious to the ground. Men of King Yder's household, carrying him to his quarters, were met by a messenger from the queen, who asked that he be brought to her chambers instead. He had lost so much blood it seemed certain that he would die, but skillful doctors, and the women's care, would restore him to life, if not to health.

Meanwhile, the Britons, led by Yvain, chased the surviving Saxons back into their citadel. They themselves dared not approach too closely, because arrows were constantly flying from the battlements. Nor was there any way to surround Saxon Rock, on account of marshlands behind it, stretching as far as the eye could see. The knights inside no longer dared to come out and attack their enemies, although they found ways of informing allies of their plight. But King Arthur's forces also grew, as word of his imprisonment spread to his distant vassals.

℄ Lancelot, in a prison cell with seven ordinary foot-soldiers, refused to eat or drink; no attempt to console him brought any comfort. His mind, empty of all but grief and rage, gave way to such violent madness that no one could withstand him. The jailor felt pity for his plight, but when he began inflicting serious wounds on those around him, he had to be put in a cell by himself. Galehaut begged to be allowed to stay with him, but the jailor refused, afraid he would be killed.

Galehaut persisted. "Don't be concerned about that, my friend. I would rather be killed by him than remain alive without him."

Nothing availed. Meanwhile, the chatelaine of Saxon Rock heard about the mad prisoner. Thinking him an irksome burden – no doubt impossible to ransom, besides – she told the jailor to open the gate closest to where the Britons were encamped, and release him.

"Let him go?" exclaimed Galehaut on learning that Lancelot had been freed. "But in his madness that's sure to be the death of him!" And he almost lost his own sanity to that agonizing thought. Without his brilliant young companion, he felt that the very foundation of his existence would crack and fall apart.

℄ Outside, Lancelot rushed about wildly, terrifying every-one by his behavior, until he came to the queen's lodgings and she saw him through the window: a madman pursued by a crowd of soldiers. Guenevere shouted to the Lady of Male-haut, "Lancelot is out there – he has gone mad!"

"Perhaps that's just a ruse so that he can see you. Or if it's true, we will nurse him back to health. I'll go to him right now."

When Blaye tried to take his hand, the madman picked up stones to throw at her. She screamed, and the queen cried out that he must stop. He did so instantly, sitting down on the ground and hiding his eyes with his hands as if he were ashamed. Blaye did not dare approach him again, but when Guenevere came and took his hand, he stood up and followed her calmly into the large house. She led him to an upstairs room, where as long as she stayed with him, he was quiet. Her ladies were disturbed to see how agitated he became when the queen was not there; no one else could do anything to help him. Guenevere sent for Lionel, but even he was at risk – the madman charged him, and she had to step between them.

So she alone took care of Lancelot. Every evening she had the candles and torches put out early, because the light, she said, made him uneasy. Then she lay beside him all night long, grieving so it seemed she would die. Everyone assumed she was weeping for the king. A week went by without change. The Saxons, receiving reinforcements from the south, had begun to attack the Britons again, and the queen, seeing their ever-increasing numbers on the battlefield, became afraid.

One morning, when Lancelot was sleeping more peacefully than usual, she could not refrain from giving words to her sorrow: "What a pity that the flower of knighthood lies here helpless! How quickly you would have made an end to this war!"

At that the knight awoke and leapt to his feet. The shield that had been sent by the Lady of the Lake – the shield once split, now whole – was hanging on the wall. He seized it and put his head and arms through its straps. Then he ran to take an old lance from the rack near the door, and hurled it against a stone column in the middle of the room. The metal tip shattered. Lancelot collapsed and lost consciousness.

When he opened his eyes again, he saw the queen's face leaning over him. "Dear sweet friend," she said, "do you know me?"

"I know you, my lady, and now I can die happy."

"Do you remember how you were captured and held at Saxon Rock?"

"Why am I not still there?" he cried. "What has happened to King Arthur? And where is Galehaut? Who put this shield around my neck – I can't bear it!"

She helped him take it off, and instantly he jumped up and began to race around the room, as mad as before. He opened the door and ran out into the great hall, terrifying everyone, until finally he was overpowered and locked into a small room. The servants who hurried to the queen found her bewildered and close to collapse.

◖ Downstairs, a tall and beautiful woman had just ridden up to the house and dismounted. She was dressed in dazzling white and was escorted by two ladies, three knights, and a squire for each of them. She went directly up to the chambers where the queen, roused by the sounds of arriving guests, dried her eyes and came to welcome her. They sat down on a low couch to talk. Lancelot, out of his senses, was hammering on the heavy door of the room where he was confined, and no one had any desire to let him out. The visitor asked about the noise, and the queen could not keep herself from weeping as she said, "That was the best of all the knights in the world, but now he has gone mad and turns on everyone."

"Have someone unlock the door for me. I have come here to see him."

The peremptory statement caught the queen by surprise, and she made no protest. As soon as the door was opened, Lancelot tried to rush out, but the lady caught him by the hand, calling him "my prince" as she used to do when he was a child and lived in her magical kingdom beneath the lake. As soon as he heard the name, he stopped, looking embarrassed and confused. She asked that someone bring her the shield. "Ah, my dear prince," she said to him, "I have been so worried about you, I've come this very long way to restore you to health." Then she put the shield around his neck again, and he allowed it, remaining calm. She had him lie down on the bed, and he looked at her and knew her; then he began to weep.

The queen marveled at all this, wondering who the newcomer could be. Lancelot, in his right mind again, wanted the visitor to remove the shield, but she would do so only in her own time. She called to one of her attendants and had her take a jar of precious ointment from a jewel case. With that she rubbed Lancelot's wrists, his forehead, and the top of his head. As soon as she had finished, he fell asleep.

Turning to the queen, she said, "I'll leave you now, my lady; may God protect you. Take care that the knight not be disturbed; let him sleep as long as he can. Then have a bath prepared for him, and once he is in the water, he'll be entirely well. Advise him that this is the only shield he should carry in battle, for it is powerful against sorcery."

"Please, my lady, before you leave, tell me who you are, and how it is that you've come from so far away to help this knight."

"I have known him all his life, ever since his father died and he was left without home or lands. It was I who raised him until it was time for me to present him to King Arthur and have him made a knight."

The queen ran to embrace her, saying, "You are the Lady of the Lake! Dear friend, I beg you to stay with me and our knight a little longer! I love and honor you for saving him, and I am grateful to you also for sending the shield, with its true prediction."

"I regretted the part of my message that said I knew your very thoughts and fully shared them, because both of us loved the same person. I hope you were not distressed by such presumption. My love for Lancelot is like a mother's for her child. I rescued him from poverty and misfortune when he was still a baby, so that he would fulfill his destiny as a knight of extraordinary prowess. When he became a young man, with the beauty and strength you saw in him when he first came to court, I could no longer keep him with me. Foreseeing all that was to happen, I sent the shield where he would know a woman's love."

She went on. "Before I leave, there is something I want to say to you, because I hold you dear. The greatest knight ever seen, the most valiant and noble, loves you with all his heart. Love him as he loves you. Keep faith with him as he will keep faith with you. Let no thought of rank come between you, or concern for what those around you think of as honor; he wants nothing, cares for nothing, besides you. Your love may be sin and madness, but let it be what you live for, since the one you love has no peer. By this, you have much to gain – first, the very flower of knighthood, and second, my friendship, for whatever it may be worth to you. Those who truly love find joy only in their beloved, and what can we place above the source of joy?"

The two women felt great affection for each other. They spoke for a long time, but when it began to grow dark, the queen saw that her guest was intent on leaving. So they bade each other farewell, and the Lady rode away with her retinue.

Guenevere, happier than she had been for days, went back to where Lancelot was sleeping, and watched over him until he awoke. Then he complained of feeling weak, but added, "I don't know why." She thought it best to wait until he was completely cured before recounting what had happened. She had a bath prepared, and she and her ladies gently helped him to get in. His beauty and strength were restored to him in an instant.

Then she told him that he had been out of his senses, to such a degree that no one was safe from him except herself "and the Lady of the Lake, who raised you. If she hadn't come, you would never have been cured." He said that he had been aware of her presence, but thought it was a dream. The queen laughed at that, but Lancelot, ashamed to have been seen behaving in a dreadful way, feared that Guenevere would love him less, although that was not within her control, even had she desired it. She told him he had no cause for concern because "my dear, sweet friend, as God is my witness, you have more power over me than I have over you, and I am more truly yours than you are mine – not just for now but as long as there is a soul within my body."

So Lancelot's health was restored, and all the joys that are the privilege of lovers were his. For nine days he lived a life of perfect happiness. He became more beautiful than ever, and the queen loved him so much she could not imagine being without him. She was even sorry to see him so spirited and full of strength, thinking that she would die if he left the court. She sometimes wished he were a little less valiant.

❡ Fighting had been proceeding all this time, and the Britons had done very well, considering that they had no leader, but on the ninth day the sounds of warfare were close enough to be heard in the queen's lodgings. The Saxons and Irish had attacked in great numbers, trying to drive the Britons far enough from Saxon Rock so the king and his companions could be taken where no one would find them. Lancelot rushed to the window, and what he saw made him turn to the queen and ask that she give him leave to join the battle. She replied that he wasn't yet well enough, "and our side isn't losing."

"Then promise that I can go if things get worse."

To this she agreed, although much against her inclination. Lancelot was elated, and silently prayed that God would soon let the Saxons have the upper hand.

"Since we have no way of knowing what will happen, I would ask you, my lady, to have armor and weapons brought for me."

This was done. She had found for him armor that belonged to King Arthur, and he put it on. He looked ready now to overcome the fiercest of warriors.

Just then, a knight rode into the courtyard with a message for the queen. His helmet had been destroyed, and he had a deep wound in his head. There was blood all over his shoulders and his chest. Guenevere wanted to send for a doctor at once, but he knelt before her and said, "My lady, I bring you greetings from my lord Yvain. He believes that there are still some knights who have not joined the battle, and they are sorely needed. He had to send out two hundred yesterday to ward off a Saxon attack."

"Does that mean we are losing?"

"My lady, we are lost if help doesn't come. The two hundred knights who are guarding the water gate have the worst of it, trying to keep the Saxons from taking King Arthur away. They've been attacked from two sides, and many of them are dead or have had their horses killed."

Lancelot exclaimed, "I must go to them, my lady. Now is my time!"

Guenevere had a new helmet brought for the wounded knight, and told him that help was on its way. He rode off much more hopeful than he had come. Lancelot sent for Lionel, armed him as well as he could, and good horses were brought for the two of them. When it was time for Lancelot to lace up his helmet, the queen took him in her arms and kissed him with all the tenderness she felt. Then she laced the helmet for him, commending him to God that he be saved from death or captivity.

With Lionel carrying the queen's pennon on his lance, they set out. When Yvain saw in the distance the bright blue pennon with its golden crowns, he shouted to his men, "My lords, help is coming! Take heart! Fight on like the true knights you are!"

Shouting the ancient war-cry of King Arthur's clan, Lancelot and Lionel galloped up and threw themselves into the thickest of the fray. The greatest warrior who ever lived was everywhere at once, never stopping, his charger's hooves barely skimming the ground; in front of him or behind him, no one escaped his weapon. He was himself the war-flag of the army. Every knight felt protected by Lancelot's shield, defended by his sword. Like a lion, invincible, in a field of frightened deer, he was all that his foes could see, wherever they looked, and those who followed him took on his aspect. The great battalions of Irish and Saxon warriors, who had already been enjoying their victory, began to make way before him. Having believed, with the capture of its king, that Britain was theirs, they now thought themselves fortunate if they could flee the field alive.

Few indeed escaped. Yvain, elated by the marvels he was witnessing, followed close behind Lancelot, thinking him truly a king of kings. The rest of the Britons were so transformed that the weakest among them proved capable of deeds they themselves would have thought reserved for heroes. Lancelot recognized Hargadabran, the leader of the enemy, a giant of a man, whose helmet shone like a beacon high above the rest. This was Gamille's brother, the noblest of all the Saxons and the worthiest of lords – if only he hadn't coveted King Arthur's throne. It was for the sake of his ambition that Gamille had used her sorcery to seduce and betray the king. The Saxon tried to escape, but his horse was too slow; he tried to shelter beneath his shield, but Lancelot's blow sent half of it flying, and the sword cut through his thigh, and on through the saddle. Man and horse crashed to the ground in a heap as Lancelot galloped on without looking back, seeking more work for his weapon. But the enemy soldiers, now completely demoralized by the loss of the one they had counted on to protect them, were scattered and fleeing. Yvain had seen Hargadabran fall, and went to take him prisoner. When he saw the extent of the wound, he crossed himself in awe, thinking that any warrior who could strike such a blow was no mere man but an agent of God's justice. Hargadabran was taken to the tents, but there he stabbed himself to death rather than go on living, maimed.

℺ Most of the Britons remained with Yvain, while Lancelot and Lionel, sparsely accompanied, rode on. Their enemies were so frantic to escape that many lost their way and drowned in the marshes, while large numbers of others, crowding onto the causeway that led to Saxon Rock, were trampled by their comrades. Lancelot, far in the lead on his swift horse, was about to charge into the struggling throng, when Lionel arrived and desperately tried to turn him back. Already a large crowd of Saxons had turned around to see the one man advancing against their army. Their terror was so great that they froze in place, but Lionel seized the bridle of Lancelot's horse. Furious, Lancelot made him let go and spurred forward. But when Lionel shouted at him to stop "in the name of the queen! Don't throw away your life!" Lancelot reined in his horse and stood still.

Yvain and his men were just reaching the causeway, but, numerous as they were, he judged it imprudent to pursue the enemy further along that narrow road. Lancelot, however, rode away alone, greatly distressed by being forced to withdraw. On the other side of Saxon Rock, facing the British camp, he found an entrance protected by a magic wall of air. Powerful against enchantments, his shield enabled him to ride straight through. Once inside, he continued on horseback through room after empty room until he came to the great hall where many men were hastily arming themselves, having heard about the defeat of their allies. Lancelot galloped into their midst, and the few who escaped were barely able to take refuge inside the stone tower.

Covered with blood, on foot and with sword in hand, Lancelot searched the castle until he found Gamille in the arms of her lover, now doomed. Slaying the man, he seized the lady, threatening to cut her throat unless she took him to where the king and the other prisoners were being held. He also forced her to open a storeroom full of weapons.

King Arthur had no idea to whom he owed his sudden liberation. He and Guerrehet hastened to arm themselves, and went with Lancelot to free Galehaut and Gawain. Galehaut, however, refused to take part in their rejoicing, saying that he had no desire to fight, no reason to live, since Lancelot was dead.

"Ah, my dear friend, you are wrong! I am here!" The young

knight took off his helmet, and Galehaut rushed to embrace him.

Gawain turned to the king, saying, "My lord, this is the knight we have sought so long – the Red Knight and then the Black! He is Lancelot of the Lake, the man who made the peace with Galehaut."

Arthur fell at Lancelot's feet, and said, "My lord, henceforth my life, my honor, and my lands are in your power, since I owe them all to you." Lancelot, with tears in his eyes, raised him up. The king should not kneel before him. Besides, there was more to do.

They made their way to the tower. The knights inside refused to open the door, but when Lancelot threatened to kill their lady, they agreed to surrender, provided the king let them go free. Arthur consented, and soon his banner flew in triumph over Saxon Rock. The sight was an immense relief to those in the British camp, and especially to the queen who had believed that Lancelot must be dead. She had nearly died herself, so great was her anguish.

Soon all the knights were racing toward the fortress. There Sir Kay discovered a maiden who had spent the last three years in irons, for the crime of having made Gamille jealous. On being released, however, the girl seemed anxious rather than jubilant. She pressed the seneschal to tell her whether Gamille was still in the castle. "My lord," she urged him, "you must destroy her books of magic! With them she can make water flow uphill! Your triumph would be for naught." She showed

Kay a chest full of strangely inscribed books and some loose pages that bore characters and signs he had never seen before. He hauled the sinister load to a parapet high in the fortress and burned it without a moment's hesitation. Gamille, discovering her irreplaceable volumes reduced to ashes, ran to the edge of the parapet and hurled herself to the ground below. To her lasting shame, she did not die, but lived out her life grotesquely crippled. King Arthur, saddened by her plight and still in thrall to her beauty, did not cease to love her.

❡ So Saxon Rock was taken. Sir Gawain warned the king that he risked losing Lancelot once again, if he didn't take care, because "Galehaut is more possessive of him than a knight with a beautiful lady, and he will want to take him away."

The victorious knights gathered in the great hall of the castle. The queen arrived, and everyone ran to greet her, but she went straight to Lancelot and threw her arms around his neck and kissed him. She intended by this to show that there was nothing improper between them, and all who saw her gesture honored her for it. But Lancelot felt troubled. Sensing this, she said in a voice that all could hear, "My lord knight, I regret that I do not know who you are, nor how I can reward you for your deeds today. You have saved the king's honor and my own, and for your perfect loyalty, I grant you my true love."

The king thought she could not have spoken better. Guenevere went to offer words of praise to the other knights in the hall, and then she told how she had found the unknown knight raving mad, and how he had been made well by one who was called the Lady of the Lake.

"My lady," said the king, "the name of this knight is Lancelot, and it is he we have been seeking for so long! It is he who won the day in my two battles with Galehaut."

The queen looked convincingly astonished, so much so that even Gawain was almost taken in. She listened with delight while Yvain told how Lancelot's prowess had defeated the Saxon hordes. "We had hoped for reinforcements, but even with the two hundred men we lacked we would never have won the victory this one knight achieved all by himself!"

"How could I not prize him over all other knights!" exclaimed the king. "He rescued me from captivity, and won for me the very fortress that cost me so much suffering!"

Galehaut spoke quietly to Lancelot. "My dear friend," he said, with a deep sigh, "the time has come when I must lose you."

"How is that, my lord?"

"What shall I do when the king asks you to join the Round Table? You are all the world to me, and you know that I am yours, in heart and soul."

"You are the worthiest man I have ever seen or known, and my love is wholly yours. Why would I want to join King Arthur's household?"

"But if the queen asked...?"

"I would refuse her if I could."

"We both know that would be impossible."

That evening, the king took Guenevere aside and told her that he wanted to keep Lancelot beside him as a knight of the Round Table.

"You must ask Galehaut if he will allow that, my lord," she answered, "since Lancelot and he are sworn companions."

So Arthur put his proposal to Galehaut, who replied that he had subordinated his own interests to the king's for the love of Lancelot, "and now, if you take him from me, you will be taking my life. I cannot live without him." He said this hoping that the queen would not intervene.

But the king looked at her, saying, "Ask him for me," and Guenevere fell to her knees.

Lancelot could not bear to see her thus, and without consulting Galehaut, cried, "Ah, my lady! I will stay with the king if that is what you desire." He raised her up, and she thanked him from her heart.

Galehaut said to Arthur, "I would rather be poor and happy than rich and miserable! If I have ever done anything that pleased you, I ask you to retain me as well. I ask you this for both of us, and I remind you that my love for him is the source of my love for you." The king leapt to his feet, embraced Galehaut, and said that both of them could stay, not merely as his knights, but as his companions and his peers.

℄ King Arthur held high court there in Saxon Rock for seven days, during which time the festivities in honor of Lancelot and of Galehaut never ceased. It was a noble and splendid week, a week of jousts and games and music, culminating on All Saints' Day. That morning, after mass, the two companions took their seats at the Round Table, and learned clerks were summoned to record how the fortress had been taken, so that the knowledge of Lancelot's extraordinary feats would not be lost. Jongleurs sang of his valor.

The king was happy in the knowledge that the allegiance of the greatest defender of his realm was henceforth firmly assured. But there was something deeper. From the time the youth had come to him, all clad in white, handsome and high-minded, eager for renown, he had felt drawn to him almost as a father to a son. Lancelot was everything that Arthur would have wanted in his heir. Seeing him now, a companion of the Round Table, gratified him profoundly.

The queen, for her part, was more than content, for she had not only secured her love but sheltered it behind the face of propriety and honor. Lancelot, experiencing the joy and gratitude of the court, felt elated. He had set out along his path with the matchless help of the Lady of the Lake and been drawn forward by the power of his love for the queen. The prowess that the two women had inspired in him was made manifest in the White Knight who had conquered Dolorous Guard, the Red Knight who had held back Galehaut's battalions, the Black Knight who had transformed a sure defeat into victory. But through it all he had been only Lancelot of the Lake; recognized now in his true identity, he felt, at last, worthy of his kingly heritage. In all the excitement of the moment, he never ceased to remember his companion, although the thought was edged with a vague unease. For Galehaut was indeed the least enthusiastic witness to the week's triumph, and all his brave efforts to share in the general delight could not wholly mask the trouble in his heart.

At last, leaving a garrison to hold Saxon Rock, the Britons made their way slowly back to their homeland. When they reached Carleon, Galehaut took leave of the king, asking him to allow Lancelot to accompany him to Sorelais. Reluctantly, Arthur gave permission; they would rejoin him at Camelot in time for Christmas.

LANCELOT AND THE LORD
OF THE DISTANT ISLES

❖   ❖   ❖

PART TWO

BOOK EIGHT ✦ THE FATE OF GALEHAUT

AS THEY RODE AWAY, GALEHAUT, happy that Lancelot had agreed to return home with him, was nevertheless convinced that his companion, now a member of the Round Table, would be lost to him in the end. And he had given him his heart with a love greater than a father's for his son, or a brother's for a brother; he knew he could not survive their separation. He was twenty-two when he had become a knight – would he live to see his fortieth year? Galehaut realized that his reputation for prowess and great deeds placed him second only to King Arthur, though some proclaimed him to be in truth more valiant still. Before meeting Lancelot, he had shown an ambition, skill, and courage unequaled by any king on earth. He had wished to embrace the whole world with his conquests, and surely he would have done so. Had it not been for Lancelot, Arthur would have fallen just like the thirty other kings who had become his vassals. But in surrendering when he had, in fact, triumphed, he had hardly traded victory for a shameful peace, as some men were quick to claim. To them, as to himself, he could only reply that nothing he had ever done seemed as honorable as that decision, "because a valor beyond any other the world has seen is a miraculous gift," and Galehaut could only bow before the wishes of the man who embodied that valor. He saw as wisdom what others viewed as folly, as gain what others considered loss. No one else could even imagine a love as great as his.

The further they rode away from Carleon, the more Lancelot felt his separation from the queen. He grieved, too, for Galehaut, knowing that he had joined the Round Table against his will, and only for the sake of their friendship. They rode mainly in silence, each fearing to hurt the other if they spoke of what was closest to their hearts. But the greater sorrow was Galehaut's. Lancelot would surely see the queen again. He was longing for her already. Sooner or later he would be lost to the companion who loved him more than life itself. Even now, with Lancelot right beside him, Galehaut felt that joy was no longer possible.

℄ That night they stayed at a castle on the opposite side of the Severn from Sorelais. Galehaut felt ill, having eaten almost nothing during the journey. He appeared to be cheerful enough through the evening, but later, in bed, Lancelot could hear him weeping, and many times he cried out in his sleep that he was betrayed. The next day he rode with his head down, urging his horse to greater and greater speed over rough paths – until it stumbled against a rock and fell, flinging Galehaut to the ground. He lay motionless, blood running from a deep gash in his forehead. Lancelot, thinking he might be dead, leapt from his horse and threw himself over his friend, nearly unconscious himself in the intensity of his emotion. The four squires who accompanied them believed that both were lost.

But then Lancelot heard Galehaut's deep sigh, and, in his relief, reproached his friend for riding so wildly – only by luck was he still alive!

Galehaut replied, "I have been lucky indeed, my whole life long, and God has granted me everything I desired. A man who has everything can be given no more, he can only lose. Even as I have fallen today, I have gone from winning to losing." That pronouncement, in its implacable clarity, struck Lancelot like a blow.

One of the squires tore a strip from his tunic to improvise a bandage for Galehaut. His horse had a bruised knee, but could still be ridden. As they continued their journey, Lancelot said, "There must be something more that you are not saying. You know I would do anything to help you."

"I'll tell you what I never thought to speak of to anyone. I have had two dreams which frighten me still. In one, I thought I saw myself at Arthur's court with many other knights. An enormous serpent came out of the queen's room straight toward me. Long flames darted from its mouth and burned off my legs. Then last night I dreamed that I had two hearts in my chest, and they were exactly alike. As I looked at them, one of them left my body and turned into a leopard. It joined a great company of beasts as wild as itself. Then my heart and my whole body turned dry as dust, and it seemed to me that I was dying. These dreams have never left my thoughts, and I can't rest until I find out what they mean."

"My lord," said Lancelot, "you are much too wise to be

troubled by such dreams! The most powerful man in the world has nothing to fear!"

"There is only one man I fear, and should he wish to harm me, nothing would help or save me."

℃ Once they had crossed the bridge into Sorelais, Galehaut took a righthand path leading to a castle of his, built on solid rock, high on a hill, with a swiftly-flowing river below it. For its strength and beauty, he had given it the name of Proud Fortress, and it was here that he had once planned to imprison King Arthur. From a league or so away, they had a view of its high tower and the strong walls with their formidable battlements. Lancelot said, "That is the most impressive castle I've ever seen! It must have been built with lofty purposes in mind!"

"Dear friend, dear companion, let me tell you how true that is! When I began it, my goal was to be the ruler of the entire world. If I tell you the truth about it, you'll know the proud height from which I have fallen, for much of what I so arrogantly hoped to do has remained unaccomplished. There are exactly one hundred and fifty crenels in the battlements, because I intended to turn one hundred and fifty kings into my vassals. When I had conquered all of them, I planned to bring them here to this castle, and then I would sit on a royal throne surrounded by all those crowned kings, there to do me honor. I would at last be crowned myself and would hold court in a manner befitting so great a ruler; I would be remembered after my death. I have always left this castle happier than when I came, but this time that is very unlikely to happen."

Lancelot listened and said nothing, thinking to himself, "How he should hate me for all these things I've prevented him from doing! The most powerful man in the world has lost all his ambition, because of me." He turned his head away, so that Galehaut would not see the tears filling his eyes.

By then they had climbed until they were very close to the castle. It was utterly silent. No one came to greet them; there was no watchman on top of the tower. The drawbridge, missing a number of planks, was lowered, as if defense were no longer important. Galehaut and Lancelot made their way across, passed through the unmanned barbican, reached the final gate, which sagged and swung on its hinges. They looked inside. The great courtyard was cluttered with stones; large sections of the inner walls had fallen. Outside, the travelers saw that the masonry was cracked, and clearly, it was only a matter of time before the tower itself would collapse. Galehaut was struck dumb. He turned his horse's head and galloped back the way they had come, with Lancelot close behind him, trying to imagine words of comfort. When Galehaut finally slowed down, Lancelot said, "My lord, I know a man as noble as you can't really be troubled by such a loss, so long as he and his friends remain unharmed."

Galehaut smiled ruefully at this. "Do you think that I am grieving for my castle? If you understood me better, you would realize that I have never been concerned about lands or wealth. Even when I wished to conquer great kingdoms and hold their rulers under my sway, my purpose was not mere possession. What I sought was glory. And now I have been glad to cast it aside. All my conquests only left me with a need to go beyond, to discover what more might be possible. Had I defeated King Arthur, which then seemed the summit of my ambitions, the result would have been the same. But once I saw you on the battlefield, everything changed. All that has mattered to me since that moment has been your friendship, worth more than all the kingdoms of the world. Yet the ruin of Proud Fortress confirms my heart's foreboding. This is a sign; it is the beginning of the end of my happiness."

"Doesn't it often happen," asked Lancelot, "that such foreboding comes from sickness in the body? And you have not been well these many days. Remember that no one on earth is strong enough to do you harm."

"Only two men have brought fear to my heart. One is you, and the other is myself. If one or the other of us met misfortune, the result, for me, would be the same. My love for you is such that I would pray God not to let me live a single day beyond the day of your death. The only thing I fear is losing you, whether by death or through another kind of separation. Dare I say it? If my lady the queen were as generous to me as I have been to her, she would not deprive me of your company. She would remember that I made possible what she so greatly desired and what brought you such joy. Yet it probably isn't fair to blame her for preferring her own heart's pleasure to that of another. She once told me that you can't make a gift of something unless you know how to give it up, and I've learned how true that is. But, in the end, I only want you to know that if I should lose your company, the world will lose mine."

"My dear lord, please God we never need to separate! You have done so much for me that I couldn't bear to cause you pain. If I joined King Arthur's household it was only because of my lady – in my heart I didn't want to."

⦅ They talked for a long time, and gradually Galehaut began to feel less oppressed. He suggested that they leave the ruin of Proud Fortress and ride toward the castle of Tessaline, which was close to a river and surrounded by beautiful meadows. On the way, they would stay in a monastery overnight, and the squires were sent ahead to prepare their accommodations. The two knights traveled more slowly, Galehaut finding solace in the undisturbed serenity of the forest, the golden light of autumn lending a kind of harmony to his thoughts. They spent the day in pleasant conversation, and it was almost dark when they arrived. The fact that the Lord of the Distant Isles was traveling almost alone astonished the monks, for they were accustomed to seeing him always with a great retinue of knights. That evening Galehaut ate more than he had eaten since leaving Arthur's court.

The next day, when they were still a few leagues from Tessaline, Galehaut stopped at a manor house to see his childhood tutor, who was the steward of his lands and a kinsman. The man, as staunch and faithful a retainer as could be, began to weep at the sight of Galehaut. When he had somewhat recovered, and was urged to speak the truth no matter what it might be, he told how the castle, which had been flawless and beautiful, was strangely changed. It looked the same from a distance, but no one was living there because all the walls were crumbling, and stones were falling everywhere. Even the castle at Sorham, the main city of Sorelais, was threatened.

Galehaut received this news with equanimity, saying that since he had been given a heart capable of the highest deeds, he should surely have the courage to make the best of misfortune. Castles, after all, were only material things, and no lives had been lost. He and Lancelot rode on to Sorham where servants, notified of his coming, were able to welcome him suitably. But the cracks in the walls foretold the castle's fate.

℄ Galehaut spoke again to Lancelot of his terrible dreams, saying he was determined to send for a wise man to explain them. Lancelot wondered whether any such person could help, but King Arthur had told Galehaut of his own experience with Master Elias: how that interpreter had found a warning in his dreams, the warning that, without greater generosity, he would lose his kingdom. "These dreams," said Galehaut, "must be tied to you and to my life with you. I need to learn what they mean." He dispatched a messenger to Arthur, asking him to send Master Elias to Sorham.

He was a long time in coming, although the king summoned him as soon as he had heard Galehaut's request, but

Master Elias was an aged man and it was hard for him to travel. Galehaut and Lancelot spent the days as best they could, taking stock of the damage, wondering how to repair one wall while pretending another was not almost as badly fissured, all the time trying to seem confident that the future would go well, each for the sake of the other. Yet each of them knew, in his heart, that nothing could really be done. The cracked walls and weakened towers were only the visible signs of a force that had eroded Galehaut's great and realizable aspirations, the ambitions that had formed the very substance of his life.

When a servant announced that Master Elias had arrived, Galehaut made haste to welcome him and thank him for coming. "I am grateful to you, and also to King Arthur, who sent you here to help me in my need. I know that he considers you the wisest man in his realm and holds you in great esteem. I need nothing in the world more than the good counsel you can give. I have lands and wealth enough to befit a man much worthier than myself, and I have good and valiant friends. But all my riches do nothing to help me, indeed they do me harm, by reason of their very uselessness."

Master Elias's silence invited Galehaut to go on. "I suffer from a malady different from any other, since I feel it isn't truly lodged within my flesh or bones. Some kind of sickness has made its way into my heart, and it is destroying me. I have lost all appetite for food and drink, and when I lie in my bed I cannot sleep. I think that it may have come from a certain fear I have, but possibly the fear has come from the illness, since both began at about the same time. That is why I have such great need of your advice. Counsel me, for the love of God – and for the love of King Arthur, too, and because your help will win you my lasting friendship."

Master Elias replied, "There are three illnesses that affect the heart, and none of them can be cured by medicines for the body. Sometimes the cause is a sin which can only be atoned for by prayers and fasting and almsgiving, as the men of religion advise. Sometimes a person has been wronged and can never be at ease until the injustice is brought to light and he is avenged. But the worst of these maladies, and the hardest to cure, is caused by love. Only refined and sensitive hearts are vulnerable to love, which invades them through the eyes and the ears. When that happens, the lover cannot do otherwise than chase after his quarry, and if he is successful, he will be cured; otherwise, he will die. He'll be held captive, just as if he had not caught his prey, although his prison is not without its comforts. He can hear the sweet words and enjoy the company of his beloved, and the prospect of having all his desires fulfilled. But he also suffers from the fear of losing what he loves, afraid that he may be harmed by false accusations. What makes this third malady so dangerous is that oftentimes the suffererer does not want to be cured, preferring the illness to good health." He paused for a moment.

"Because you told me that yours is a sickness of the heart, I have described the three types that exist. Yours must be one of the three. So now please tell me about your condition and how you feel. If my knowledge can be of use, I will be more than glad to help you."

"Dear Master," said Galehaut, "even if you were to tell me no more than you have already done, I would be ready to place my life in your hands. But before I describe the nature of my illness, and tell you how it began, I must ask you to swear on holy relics that you will never reveal to anyone what I say, and that you will tell me the truth without concealing anything, no matter now painful it may be."

When the oath had been sworn, Galehaut recounted the two dreams that had frightened him so much. Afterwards, Master Elias said that such dreams could not be hastily explained, but required that the interpreter meditate on them at length until he saw their deepest meaning. He asked to be given a room where he could spend the night in solitary contemplation.

The next morning he met with Galehaut in a chapel; no one else was there except Lancelot. Master Elias said, "You dreamed of a leopard who took your heart and a serpent who deprived you of your limbs. The serpent is the queen. She made it impossible for you to move, and she alone can prevent the leopard from taking your life. After the lion, which always represents a king, the leopard is the greatest of all animals. The leopard in your dream is the greatest knight in the world." He hesitated before continuing. "I had a vision during the night, a vision of a bridge of forty-five planks spanning a dark river. But I can relate that to you only when we are alone."

"Won't you allow my companion to hear it also?"

"My lord, a treatment must be given in the way that will do most good, rather than as the patient might prefer. If you want to profit from my knowledge, you will have to obey me in this."

Then Galehaut looked at Lancelot, who rose immediately and left the chapel. He was overcome with grief, because, despite all his resistance to the idea, he knew that he himself must be the deadly leopard. How could it be otherwise? And it was strange to him that Galehaut seemed not to understand. He went into a small side room, closed the door behind him, and wept as if his heart would break. At last, not wanting Galehaut to see him in such a state, he decided to take a walk along the battlements.

❡ Meanwhile, Master Elias was assuring Galehaut that he recognized him as among the wisest men in the world, that whatever follies he had committed, he had acted more out of generosity of heart than through lack of understanding. "Because of that, I want to offer this useful counsel: take care not to let someone you truly love hear anything that could cause anger or distress. I say this because of the knight who left just now. I know you love him with the greatest love there can be between two companions, and that you wanted him to be here while I spoke with you. But he might have heard something that would cause him shame and sorrow, and he would perhaps have suffered more from this than you will.

I know that you care for his happiness and well-being as much as he does himself, but it is also true that he does not see his way as clearly as you do yours."

"Master, it seems you know us very well," said Galehaut. "Will you tell me about the vision you had last night?"

"You were crossing a bridge originally made of forty-five planks. But deep water extended far beyond the last plank, because some had been removed. There you had to jump off; nor was there any way back, because the bridge had disappeared. This would surely be a vision of your death, except that it was the leopard who had taken away the planks, and the leopard could also replace them."

"But what do they mean, those forty-five planks! Are they the years of my life – and how many are missing?"

"You would be better off not thinking about that! No one born into this world would ever again have an hour of peace or happiness if he knew when he would die. Nothing is as frightening as death, and if the body's death is so dreaded, how much more awesome is the death of the soul!"

"That's exactly why I seek to know how much more time I have! If my life is to be short, I must hurry to seek forgiveness for my sins – and I need forgiveness more than most. How many cities have been destroyed to satisfy my ambition! How many men have been killed, or ruined, or sent into exile!"

"I know how great is your need, because no one who wins fame as a conqueror does so without great sin. The knowledge you seek might indeed help you to mend your ways. But it is far more likely to have the opposite effect; when all hope is lost, the door stands open to fear, and fear brings loss of faith, an invitation to the devil."

"I promise you, Master, that knowing when I must die will not make me lose hope – my faith is not so weak! God has given me wealth and honors enough to content the greatest man who ever lived, and perhaps his love will grant me not only the pleasures of this world but also never-ending happiness in the next. The closer I am to my death, the more I will strive to be worthy of that eternal reward. So I beg you to tell me everything you know. Do not refuse to help me save my soul! You will imperil your own if you keep silent or if your words lengthen the term set for my life, since the longer I think I will live, the longer will I put off atonement for my sins."

Master Elias had never heard so moving a plea for the knowledge of death. He answered, "You are right. I see I must yield to your will. I am glad to do so in one way, and regret it in another. You have so much wisdom that I believe what you ask must be for the good, but I feel a terrible grief at the thought of your death. What a loss that a man so worthy and admirable should not be given the full span of his years! I promise to tell you everything I can. I will not be able to say that you cannot live beyond a particular day, but only that that day will be the day of your death unless something happens to prevent it. And events could also hasten the coming of that day."

He took a piece of coal and drew forty-five circles on the freshly whitewashed wall of the chapel. They represented the planks of the bridge, "which stand for the years you might yet live. What I am going to do may make one or more of the circles disappear. Should that happen, your life will be shorter by that many years. Don't be startled by what you will see, although you have probably never witnessed anything so astonishing."

With that he reached into his robe and took out a little book. He opened it and said to Galehaut, "This book treats of the meaning and the mystery of all the great spells whose power is in words. Its pages will reveal what is hidden from me now. If I wished, the book would enable me to cause earthquakes, direct the winds, tame beasts in the wild. But the source of such knowledge is not to be approached lightly. Learned men have been blinded, or paralyzed, and some of them have been killed for having consulted it carelessly. I promise that you will not be unmoved by what you see."

He sat down on a stone bench and began to read. After a while his heart began to beat wildly, his face was flushed, sweat and tears mingled on his cheeks. Galehaut watched him with increasing anxiety. The master continued thus for a long time. Then he began groaning as if in pain, and his whole body trembled. A great darkness entered the room, and they were in an abyss where nothing at all could be seen. The chapel seemed to be whirling around, and Galehaut would have fallen had he not held tight to a pillar. A hideous voice was heard,

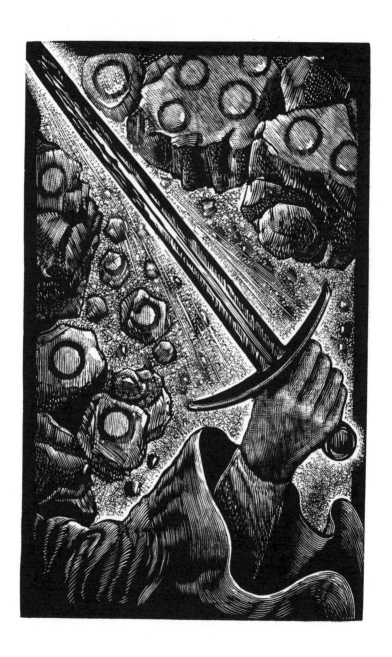

shrieking and laughing at once. Galehaut thought the sound surely reached into every corner of the city. When at last it faded away and daylight slowly returned, Galehaut found the master nearly unconscious on the ground. When he could speak, he told Galehaut to stay behind him whatever happened.

Through the closed door of the chapel came a long arm draped in purple samite from shoulder to elbow, and in white from elbow to wrist. The silken folds reached to the ground. A hand the color of glowing embers held a crimson sword dripping with blood. It flew through the air to point directly at Master Elias, but, with a prayer or an incantation, he caused it to retreat. It threatened five times to run him through, and always he drove it back. At last the sword turned, as if in rage, and slashed against the wall where the circles were drawn. The stone was so deeply cracked that a full arm's length of it fell away, taking with it forty-two of the circles. After that the apparition left the way it had come in.

Galehaut was stunned; he had never witnessed such power before. After a silence, he said to the master, "You have truly fulfilled your promise that I would be amazed. And, as I promised you, my mind is now at peace. I know that I have three years to live, and no one else could do as much good as I will do in that time. I won't live in sadness, but in greater joy than ever before."

"Let me remind you," said Master Elias, "that although I was distressed to show you what you have seen, there is a way for you to live beyond that limit, but it depends upon the queen. What Merlin prophesied so long ago is happening now. He predicted that a wondrous dragon would come from the Distant Isles. Flying left and right over many lands, the dragon would constantly grow in power as he subdued them. When he reached the kingdom of Logres, his shadow would be so vast that it would darken the whole land. By then, the dragon would have thirty heads all made of gold. Logres would have fallen as quickly as the others, had a magnificent leopard not held the invader back, putting him at the mercy of the ruler he was on the very point of defeating. Later there would be such love between the dragon and the leopard that they would feel they were one being, each unable to live without the other. But a golden-headed serpent would steal the leopard away and corrupt his heart. And that is how the great dragon would die." He paused.

"I know you are that dragon," Elias went on, "and the queen, who is the serpent in your dream, will love your companion as much as any lady can love a knight. But that will be more than you can bear, so great is your love for him."

Galehaut reflected for a moment, then answered, "I could endure it for a while, but not forever – my heart is completely in his keeping. Still, I cannot see how he would cause my death, unless by his own. The world would be empty for me without him, and I could not long survive."

"Merlin wrote of what must come, but the way it comes is hidden from our sight. I will leave you now, but remember, if you can keep your companion by your side, you will certainly pass the limit of three years – it is only for lack of him that you will die. I urge you, however, not to reveal to him or anyone else what has been said here. The truth of one's desiny is not to be shared with others."

"I will do as you advise."

⁋ Master Elias took his leave, and Galehaut remained lost in thought, images of years, like circles, whirling through his mind. The dreams had confirmed what he already knew: that his love could bring his death, and his beloved would be its instrument. But he had not imagined that death would come so soon.

Only after a while did he send for Lancelot. The young man arrived trying to look cheerful, but his eyes were red from weeping. "Well, my dear companion," said Galehaut, "I know that you have been troubled about me, but I have news that will warm your heart."

Lancelot was not immediately reassured. "Tell me what he said about the forty-five planks," he countered, "and why I had to leave the room. I'm afraid he may have wanted to speak of the queen and me."

"Nothing of the kind! He said nothing about the queen. He wanted you to leave so that I could make my confession. Otherwise he wouldn't tell me what I wanted to know. Master Elias cast a spell. He brought forth from the darkness a truth that could not be doubted. The planks represented my years to come, and he predicted I would live forty-five more." Galehaut was pained to find himself trapped into such fabrications. He had been obliged more than once to disguise his true feelings, to keep silent about matters that might disturb his companion, but those were sins of omission, if sins at all. Now, however, he felt forced into distortions and outright lies, and he detested himself for such weakness.

He went on, "What you do for me, dear friend, is beyond all gratitude. Were it not for your being here, I would have succumbed too easily to the warnings that I saw in my dreams. Perhaps I would not even have sought their true interpretation. Now we can see that there is no reason to be sad, but rather to rejoice that my fears were groundless." So Galehaut tried to find comfort for Lancelot if not for himself, and continued acting happier than he felt – all this for the sake of his companion, whose relief was evident.

S OME DAYS AFTER MASTER ELIAS'S
visit, a messenger arrived from the queen, with a terrible story to tell. Galehaut received him in private,
while Lancelot was still sleeping. A lady had come to
Arthur's court, accompanied by a large number of knights and
servants, more than thirty in all. Claiming to be the daughter
of the King of Carmelide, Guenevere's own father, she accused
the queen of being an impostor, her bastard sister adulter-
ously born to the wife of their father's seneschal. She, too, was
named Guenevere – the true one! She said that Arthur, know-
ingly or not, was living in sin, his presumed queen no more
than a concubine. According to her story, she had been married to the king in the Church of Saint Stephen the Martyr, in
the capital city of Logres. The king had had only a glimpse of
her before, and during the ceremony she was veiled. She was
conveyed to the castle separately from Arthur, who, when
they arrived, was called away for a moment. She, meanwhile,
was taken to private quarters to ready herself for what would
follow. Someone brought her spiced wine to drink, and the
next thing she knew she was being led away again, this time
in stealth, her new destination a distant manor which was, in
fact, a prison.

Years went by, she said. Her jailors were not unkind to her,
and she managed to persuade one of them to carry a message

to Bertolay the Old, the most respected and valiant knight of Carmelide, who had always known her and loved her. Bertolay rescued her and was now by her side at Arthur's court; the barons of Carmelide would surely follow his lead. She was certain of Bertolay's loyalty, unlike that of her very father, who might well have been the agent of her betrayal! Perhaps he had wanted to serve the scheming mother of her half-sister, now pretending to be the rightful queen. And against Guenevere, finally, she made a formal accusation, demanding that the king give her over to justice. The allegation astounded the king, and he commanded Guenevere to respond, but all she could say was that her defense must be her innocence itself.

Galehaut listened intently, with rising agitation, although he was inclined to think the matter inconsequential. How could Arthur pay the slightest attention to such vile slander! But the messenger assured him that the king was taking it seriously. Instead of dismissing the pretender, who seemed to have no proof of her own identity, Arthur had declared that he would hold court at Bredigan, on the border of Carmelide, and hear both sides in six weeks' time. The messenger added that King Arthur seemed to be attracted to the lady. She was very beautiful, and had made a startling impression as she strode through the crowd of knights and ladies toward the king. With her long hair in a single golden braid, shining against the crimson of her cloak, she did indeed look remarkably like the queen.

The courier went on to say that Guenevere suspected the pretender of being an agent of Arthur's sister, Morgan the Fay, who had been bitterly opposed to their marriage, and whose jealousy of the queen was such that she would do anything to ruin her. If the pretender's claim was upheld to the satisfaction of the king, the queen would be repudiated, possibly even put to death. But before that happened, Sir Gawain would insist on a trial by combat, even though he himself would not yet be well enough to fight as the queen's defender. Surely, someone worthy would be found to face the accuser's champion! Guenevere's messenger was charged to ask Galehaut and Lancelot to come to Bredigan to do what they could. Galehaut said he would give him an answer very soon, and suggested he rest and have some refreshment.

It was stunning news – very hard to believe, or to imagine. Above all, how was he to convey it to Lancelot without throwing him into a blind rage? Galehaut was at first tempted to tell him nothing at all, but then realized that news of the alleged imposture was too terrible not to travel far and fast. He could not risk letting Lancelot hear it from another source. Reluctantly he went to rouse his companion.

Lancelot was still half asleep when Galehaut walked into the room, but was instantly alert when he heard there was a message from the queen. Galehaut said it was startling. Lancelot sprang forward in expectation. It was dire, said Galehaut, and would require a measured response. Lancelot grew

166

anxious. The event could nevertheless be made to work to Lancelot's advantage, Galehaut insisted, even before recounting what had happened. That was a vain attempt to forestall the inevitable, for Galehaut himself was agitated, and his retelling of the news let loose a storm of passion, a frantic cry for combat that the older man was unable to restrain. He listened, grieved, and waited.

After a while, Lancelot, more drained than composed, sank into silence, and Galehaut could hope he would listen to reason. Yes, of course, it was a horrendous attack on the queen, and Arthur's failure to dismiss the accusation out of hand was an inexcusable second assault on her dignity. In fact, it meant her very life might be at stake. But Galehaut thought some good might come of what had happened; the intruder's slander might even have a beneficial outcome. He ventured that it might well be the best thing if the king repudiated Guenevere. "If Arthur accepts the charge of imposture and banishes her, I will not only grant her a haven in Sorelais. I will cede my power in such a way that she may effectively govern this realm. Then the two of you can be together as much as you wish, openly. Your love need no longer be a secret, and if you cared to marry, there would be no impediment. Never could she find, my dear friend, a better man than you."

"No," said Lancelot, "it won't be that simple, and we can't just stay here and assume the king will do nothing worse than cast her aside. Hope is not enough, and her message was a cry not for refuge but for rescue! The queen faces nothing short of death. Please! If you love me, come with me to Arthur's court and help me save her!" He fell to his knees before Galehaut, to whom this plea and desperate gesture were stabs he felt in his very heart. He raised the young man to his feet, and their embrace was a wordless endorsement of their covenant.

They began to consider what to do. Galehaut proposed to go in disguise to the royal court with a hundred of his best knights; they would lie in wait for an opportunity to abduct the queen and bring her back to Sorelais. Both men, however, instantly rejected such a plan for its treason and deceit. "And how do you suppose," Lancelot added, "she would react to being seized and carried off with no warning? I could never survive her anger!"

"And survive you must, if I am to go on.... You said yourself that the queen may be facing death. If her accuser can't be proven wrong, coming with us to Sorelais may be her only hope. She would find safety in a country that could be yours no less than it is mine. My kingdom," he continued, "is without an heir, and yours has long been in the hands of a usurper. I have no son to follow me as lord of Sorelais, and the man who wrested Benoic from your noble father still rules your patrimony undisturbed. I want to grant you half my dominion over the lands I hold and have you acknowledged by all my barons; I want you to receive from them the same oath of fealty they pledged to me long ago." He paused. He saw Lancelot struggling to shape a response, and he cut off the opportunity. "And then, with their help, I want us to cross the sea and take back your kingdom. Your father's death, your mother's fate, your destitution, all these crimes cry out to be avenged. Years have passed, and justice has already waited too long. Let it not wait much longer."

Now there was silence. Lancelot turned his head away, then looked slowly back with glistening eyes. "No, my lord, my dearest friend, not yet. There is nothing I can do now but try to help my lady." His words were barely audible, but Galehaut did not need to hear them. Their conversation came to an end. They both knew that whatever might come to pass in the future, the imperative they faced right now was the need to ensure Guenevere's safety. Galehaut told the waiting messenger that they would ride to Bredigan immediately, and there see how best to help the queen.

₵ With a large escort of Galehaut's knights, the two companions rode in lengthy stages to the town, close to the kingdom of Carmelide, where accusers and defenders were soon to confront each other. The new Guenevere, the would-be queen, appeared with thirty elegant attendants. The barons of Carmelide were led by Bertolay the Old who, speaking on the lady's behalf, assured the king that he had known her all the days of her life, that he had been happy when she married with such honor, but was subsequently surprised that she never invited him to visit her at court. Then, years later and to his horror, he received her message, and ultimately was able to set her free. All the barons of Carmelide supported her in her claim that the present queen was in truth her bastard half-sister, and that she herself had been betrayed and captured on the very day of her marriage to the king. She accused the present queen of willful deception, demanded to be reinstated in her rightful place, and insisted on vengeance for her years of suffering. Only Guenevere's death would suffice.

Gawain stepped forward in defense of the only queen he recognized, but Lancelot, standing next to Galehaut in a conspicuous group of angry-looking knights, rushed past him and, without asking leave to speak, accused Arthur of offending the queen's dignity by listening to such an impossible story. "How can you imagine for a single instant that this lady, your wife and queen all these years, whose goodness has been a wonder of the world, could be guilty of such an atrocious crime? If you do not reject this slander here and now, and send this impostor, this false Guenevere, back to where she came from, I will break all connection with your court! I deeply regret having ever been part of it."

The king was taken aback by his vehemence. Torn between his affection for Lancelot and the impact of this unexpected outburst, he retorted, "What proof is there of the queen's innocence? Perhaps I have been deluded all this time! I cannot simply dismiss this accusation, supported by all the barons of Carmelide, and especially Bertolay the Old, who has known Leodagan's daughter all her life!"

"Let the decision be made by God!" cried Lancelot. "I demand that there be a trial by combat! I challenge the three best knights of Carmelide to fight me all together. My victory will be proof enough of my lady's innocence."

The king objected that by the rules of such combat, no one should be required to fight against three opponents, that such a deed had never before been attempted, and that Lancelot, brave as he was, was taking on too much. But the knight was unmoved.

Although everyone who cared about Lancelot was appalled by the conditions he proposed, both sides had to agree that judicial combat offered the only hope of justice. A well-ordered appeal to the judgment of God was, after all, an obvious advance over mere undisciplined violence or arbitrary ruling, and no one, moreover, could publicly acknowledge that God might choose to remain neutral. The false Guenevere was one of those, however, who harbored a suspicion of divine indifference to knightly confrontations, so agreement was not difficult for her. Although she risked death if Lancelot succeeded, she was sure that, facing three foes, and God not withstanding, he would be defeated.

The queen, however, tried hard to dissuade him, and in the few days granted while the barons of Carmelide chose their champions, she appealed to Galehaut. Her eyes filling with tears, she said, "I need your help now more than ever, and this time I fear you may rather let me go to my fate. Against three opponents, Lancelot is sure to lose, and the king will put me to death. We can't allow him to fight for me in so unfair a way. He too can only die! "

"If you were condemned to death, my lady, I would send for my whole army, and this time we would defeat the king as we could have done before. You will be rescued, I promise you, unless I die in the attempt! And should the king cast you aside, I will give you another kingdom to rule with Lancelot beside you. I ask only that you allow me a part in your happiness."

Guenevere was too distraught to hear Galehaut's words and went on as if they had not been spoken. "I fear that the king has been inclined to believe this accusation, because he knows that all is not well between the two of us. He doesn't know how I have strayed or with whom, but he senses it – partly, I am sure, because he has been less than true himself. What is happening now is God's punishment, isn't it – God's frightful way of telling me how much I've sinned. But there is no need for me to tell you about the power of love. The most valorous knight in the world could hardly be denied."

"Be comforted, my lady! Lancelot has no doubt that the accusation is false, and he has often fought against greater odds. Neither you nor I could keep him from this combat, and, I promise you, he will not lose."

℄ Galehaut made a last attempt to reason with the king, saying that no one had ever before questioned the queen's identity. Arthur replied that he still loved the queen above all other women, but he could not imperil his soul. Even if he had sinned in ignorance, it was still a sin, and only God's decision could show him the right way now.

"Nevertheless, my lord, you said yourself that no knight should be required to fight against three to obtain proof of a person's guilt or innocence."

"Even though Lancelot has turned against me, no knight of my household is as dear to me as he is. I owe him more than I can ever repay. I could never forgive myself if he were to be killed!"

The king was clearly in conflict with himself, and Galehaut saw one final opportunity. He said, "Then could you not declare the queen innocent, as surely you must know that she is?"

"I cannot do that," he replied. "What if the accusation were true? But I will try to persuade Lancelot to accept a more equal combat."

But when the king saw the knight armed and ready on his horse, impatient for the battle to begin, he was so moved by his proud appearance and his beauty that he spoke in a different way: "Dear friend, I beg you to give up this battle, and for your sake I will put an end to the trial. I will have your opponents withdraw, and the queen will be acquitted of all that is claimed against her."

"For my sake, there is nothing you can do! This battle will not be over until my enemies are defeated or I am dead. My honor demands it, and so does the innocence of the queen."

℄ The three knights chosen to fight for the Lady of Carmelide were armed and ready. The king could not do otherwise than accept their pledges, and Lancelot's as well. The battle would take place in a field below the castle where the pretender and Bertolay stood at a window, while Guenevere watched from the battlements. Sir Gawain, Sir Kay and other knights were with her. Galehaut laced on Lancelot's helmet, and offered him his own magnificent sword. Lancelot accepted it gladly, feeling that now he would not be fighting alone. And it was fitting, he thought, to defend the queen with a sword that came, not from her, but from the great prince who had already given so much to the accused and her champion.

Then the king ordered the guards to take their places in the field, Galehaut, King Yder, Sir Yvain among them, with worthy knights from Carmelide as well. Finally, Lancelot heard the sound he had been impatient for – the ringing tones of the horn – and he spurred his horse toward the three knights advancing at a gallop.

They rode close together, but only one of them could aim directly for the center of Lancelot's shield. He had little profit from it, though, for his lance uselessly shattered, and Lancelot's struck him so hard that the tip went right through his chest and back. He was dead when he fell to the ground. Lancelot jumped his horse over the body, instantly turned and came back at an angle, so that one of the remaining knights was slightly behind the other. From the closer one, he received a glancing blow on his helmet, but, having drawn his sword, he slipped the blade through the chain mail under the man's raised arm, and he, too, lost his life. Lancelot whirled around to meet his third opponent, whose weapon struck through his shield but did not reach the hauberk. Lancelot's return blow was so powerful that it sent the knight flying back over the croup of his horse. The queen's champion rode to where he lay in a heap; he was still alive and expecting to be killed. "Don't imagine that I would dishonor myself by fighting you from horseback!" Lancelot shouted. Dismounting, he gestured to a squire to take his horse.

This last knight, Cardoas of Lanvale, was the best in Carmelide. He struggled to his feet, sword in hand, and the opponents began exchanging heavy blows. Blood from both of them ran over the field, but they fought on until mid-afternoon. By that time it was clear that Lancelot would inevitably win, but Cardoas kept hoping that luck would yet give him an advantage. Those watching admired his courage, and began to regret the loss of such a knight. The barons of Carmelide went to the king, declared their side defeated, and begged that the life of their knight be spared. Since Arthur feared that Lancelot would reject a request from him, Galehaut suggested that he ask the queen to intervene. The king hastened to do so. "Your innocence, my lady, has been proven beyond a doubt," he said, "and there is no need for this brave knight to be killed. If you spoke to Lancelot, he would surely agree to spare him."

Guenevere ran out onto the field, right up to an astonished Lancelot, and cried, "My dear friend, stop! The king has declared himself satisfied that I am innocent, and with his consent I ask you to spare this knight."

Cardoas did not insist that the fight be prolonged! He

needed help leaving the field, so serious were his wounds, but he said that to be defeated by Lancelot was an honor in itself. The squire brought Lancelot his horse, and Galehaut escorted the queen back across the field to thunderous cheers and applause. Lancelot received a hero's welcome. Three worthy knights defeated in such a short time, and it would have been shorter still, had Lancelot been less scrupulous! King Arthur himself came to hold his stirrup and would have embraced him, but Lancelot drew back.

❡ The false Guenevere and Bertolay the Old were brought before the king. They knew that by the rules they could expect to receive the punishment that would have been meted out to the queen, had she been proven guilty. And they had asked for her death. Yet Arthur was moved by the woman's beauty and by her remarkable resemblance to his true wife. Seeing how terrified she was, he said he would be lenient, but only if they told him the truth behind their deception.

"My lord," said Bertolay the Old, "this lady is more innocent than I am. Despite my age, I have not lost my ambition. One day I received a visit from Morgan the Fay. She told me that about the time King Leodagan's daughter left for Camelot, her half-sister disappeared from view. It was generally supposed that she had traveled with the queen. In fact, the girl had gone mad with rage at not being the one to wed the king, and her mother, despondent seeing the dreadful outcome of her sin, secluded herself and her daughter in a convent. In time, the seneschal's adulterous wife passed away, while her daughter languished, not truly cured, but no longer visibly mad. The venom of her envy never left her. Morgan had long been aware of the circumstances and now came to me with a scheme to put the young woman on the throne. I was easily persuaded to be her accomplice."

The king replied, "As you may know, Morgan is my sister. I have not seen her for many years, not since before my marriage, but she has always hated Guenevere. Still, I never thought she would do anything to harm her! Morgan has always been a woman of fierce powers and with a scheming mind. No doubt she worked her magic on you both. I shall send you back to her, under guard, so that she can punish your failure as she will."

With that he dismissed them and turned to Guenevere, asking her forgiveness for having allowed himself to be so dreadfully misled. "Only my soul's salvation," he said, "is more important to me than you are!"

"That is as it should be, my dear lord."

Deeply humiliated, the barons of Carmelide came to take leave of the king. No, they assured him, King Leodagan had not known their true reason for visiting Logres; it had been easy to give the ailing old man another explanation for the journey. They had themselves been tricked by the impostor. But now the whole story would come out, since they would have to account for the absence of Bertolay. They were understandably fearful of King Leodagan's reaction, but Arthur did not offer to help them in any way. Never again would the barons of Carmelide be allowed to present a case in his court.

C Gradually life in Carduel returned to normal. The queen seemed to bear her husband no ill will for his readiness to doubt her, although many thought her exceedingly charitable. Gawain, too, was soon reconciled with the king. But Lancelot remained angry, staying at court only to be close to Guenevere. Galehaut took some encouragement from his mood, and tried to interest him in the plan he himself held dear. One afternoon, as the two of them were riding in the forest nearby, they stopped to let their horses rest near a brook, glad enough to sit quietly for a while. Galehaut thought the moment propitious to speak of their future.

"By your birth," he reminded Lancelot, "you are far nobler than I am – your father was a king, and mine a poor prince. It's time that you reclaimed your inheritance. Surely you wish to be avenged on Claudas! And I want nothing more than to help you do it. You know that since I met you I have lost all desire for warfare. But this is different. Enough of my men are still here in Logres to form an army large enough to deal with Claudas, assuming we can find him. They will be as eager as I am to fight for your cause. Why should you not have lands and wealth of your own? And how can you let your mother's suffering remain unpunished?"

Lancelot was silent for a moment. It was not as if he hadn't thought about this before, especially since Galehaut had first proposed his plan to recapture Benoic. But Benoic was, for him, a foreign country. "King Ban, my father, died too soon for me to recall his face or the sound of his voice. I have no memories of my mother, only of the Lady of the Lake, my true mother, whose love and wisdom have always been with me. I can't think of myself as the son of Queen Elaine. And yet why should Claudas continue to enjoy the kingdom he stole by treachery? I know it is my duty to restore my father's honor." His voice trailed off. "But if that land were really mine, I would be obliged to live there, as its king, at least for some of the time. I would rather stay where I am!"

"Do you think the queen would not wish you to have a kingdom of your own? Wouldn't she want you to claim what is rightly yours? Or perhaps she would think that would not be to her advantage."

"I have dreamed sometimes of conquering Benoic, but not in the way that you propose. I need to do it by myself, through my prowess and my merit; I need to win by my reputation alone. That, not an army, must drive Claudas away. And, in any case, I can undertake nothing without the encouragement of my lady the queen."

"Whatever your plans," said Galehaut, "I pray that God will let me see them come to fruition. I will do what I can, even attempt to convince the queen to help – although I doubt, to tell the truth, that she would want you in a position of authority. She likes to have you accessible as you are now, and would be afraid that responsibility and power would rob her of your company. And I know your heart as well: you would hardly wish to have a measure of lordship that might compromise or diminish her love."

Lancelot sighed and answered, "You know me very well, my dearest lord."

⁋ A few days later, the queen invited Galehaut for a private conversation. She began by asking whether he thought she had been wrong to be so quickly reconciled with the king, "who, after all, showed little concern for my honor."

Galehaut reminded her of his offer to establish her in Sorelais if she had had to separate from the king, "and that would have been the happiest solution for the three of us. But once the pretender was discredited and sent away in disgrace, I think you would have been badly judged if you had refused to forgive the king."

"And now there is no way for me to accept your truly generous offer, and trade my life here as queen for a better one. Of course, if Lancelot could remain here at court..." She sighed – "But he is so stubbornly estranged from the king."

"Lancelot's heart is so true that he can forget neither an injury nor a favor, no matter how small. And he expects others to be like him. He said he had done so much in the king's service that Arthur should have welcomed the chance to do something for him in return – not that anything could be comparable to Lancelot's saving his kingdom! He should have dismissed the charges against you as soon as Lancelot asked him to!"

But Guenevere was more interested in her immediate plans than in understanding Lancelot's behavior. "I'm sure he would listen to you, as he has done in the past."

"Then as now, my lady, I would persuade him to my harm. If Lancelot were to stay here, I would have two choices. I could return to Sorelais, my own country, where I am needed, but without the pleasure I've always felt at being there. The world is empty for me without Lancelot. Or I could stay here, where everything belongs to King Arthur, and watch my companion suffer because he can be with you only now and then, and watch him waste his valor on someone else's battles."

"What would you have him do instead?"

"Concern himself with recovering his birthright! Why should Claudas continue in possession of Lancelot's lands? I have offered to be his ally in this undertaking, but he prefers to dream of one day being restored there without a fight. If this were your desire as well as mine, I'm sure he would feel differently."

"Perhaps," she replied, "this is not the time for him to be thinking of kingship" – and with that she dismissed a course of action that held no appeal for her. "Let us strike a bargain. You will try to convince him that since I do not have a grievance against Arthur, he should not either. If you are successful, Lancelot can at least come and go as he likes, without feeling as reluctant as he does now. But if the king urges him to rejoin the Round Table, I will secretly ask Lancelot not to agree."

℧ Against his will, but seeing no alternative, Galehaut began his task of diplomacy. In this he was aided by Gawain, in whom Arthur's recent conduct still rankled but who considered that since in the end no harm had been done, it was important to have harmony at court. Gawain reported that the king was deeply grieved by Lancelot's rejection and no longer took pleasure in anything. Lancelot remained adamant for a while, but when King Arthur himself pleaded to have his friendship once again, only his friendship, with no obligations of any kind, the knight was forced to yield. A great feast was held to celebrate their reconciliation. The queen and all her ladies were magnificently dressed, Guenevere in an iridescent blue tunic set off by the ermine lining of her dark purple cloak. The Lady of Malehaut was everywhere at once. The king seemed perfectly content to have Lancelot and Galehaut at his side, and asked nothing further. In any case, Guenevere, keeping her promise to Galehaut, had requested that Lancelot refuse should the king ask him to rejoin the Round Table.

Still, King Arthur had not lost sight of that much-desired possibility. Wary of approaching Lancelot directly, he appealed to the queen, who then reported their discussion to Galehaut. Arthur had asked her to speak for the throne, and when she tried to refuse, had told her that the very life of his kingdom depended on Lancelot. Without him, rulers of the unconquered border lands would feel emboldened. The knights of the Round Table had lost their confidence and sense of purpose; they could not be counted on to defend the realm themselves. The way things were, nothing prevented Lancelot from going to live in Sorelais, even if he no longer felt ill will toward the king. Should Guenevere decline to help, Arthur would consider her disloyal to him and to the realm! "What would you have me do?" she asked Galehaut, though it was hardly a question. "I know your deepest feelings, but how can I refuse my lord the king? It would truly be a kind of treason."

Galehaut was not surprised. In his heart he had always known that, sooner or later, this would happen. Guenevere promised that he and Lancelot would be as much together as they were before, but her words sounded hollow, even to herself. Although he was sure that the queen would be more than happy to have Lancelot commit himself to Arthur's household, Galehaut, fair-minded, could not, in all honesty, see how she could prevent it. Suddenly there appeared before his eyes the white wall in the chapel with three black circles left upon it, and he wondered if he would live even that long.

⸿ On Easter Sunday, after High Mass, the queen, seconded by Galehaut, brought her appeal to the recalcitrant knight. In the interest of the kingdom, in the name of the good will – indeed the love – that the king had always felt for him, in recognition of the earnest desire of Sir Gawain and all his fellow-knights at court, out of respect for her duty as queen, mindful of the great and enduring love she shared with the most valorous knight in the world, and with the assurance that he would not be separated from his companion Galehaut, she begged, even implored, Lancelot to return to his rightful place at the Round Table.

He felt himself softening at the sound of her pleading voice. He looked at the grave face of Galehaut, and their eyes locked in unspoken agreement. Lancelot, at long last, said yes.

They went before the assembled court, where Guenevere addressed a similar, although less personal, appeal to Lancelot. Without a word, he stepped forward and fell to his knees in front of the king. The great hall was utterly silent; no one breathed. Then Lancelot humbly thanked the king for the offer of friendship he had made a few weeks earlier, and expressed the wish to be seated once again at the Round Table.

King Arthur was elated by this turn of events, not imagining that it might involve any danger to himself. Galehaut was all too aware of the irony. Arthur raised the kneeling knight by the hand, kissed him on the lips, and said, "I thank you, dear friend, and welcome you back to the Round Table. I swear to you, on this holy day, that I will never more, to the best of my ability, give you cause for anger or departure from this court."

BOOK TEN ✦ THE DEATH OF GALEHAUT

IT WAS HARD FOR GALEHAUT TO endure the court's celebration at having fully regained Lancelot. He, of course, was made equally welcome, and pretended to be light-hearted, although his companion surely knew his true feelings. Several days of festivities culminated in a hunt with almost every knight in the court participating. A great boar had recently been sighted in the forest, and there was much excitement about the challenge it presented. Galehaut made the excuse of an old wound troubling him and did not take part. Lancelot rode with Gawain, Yvain, and a few others.

The morning was cool, and the paths, with the early mist just beginning to rise, looked attractively mysterious. Game was abundant, so the knights were lured in various directions. Lancelot heard a horn call from the left and thought it might mean that the boar had been spotted. Hoping to have the honor of the prize, he galloped in the direction of the sound, but saw nothing. After a while the horn sounded again, and, later on, still another time, always leading him deeper into the forest. He was about to turn back, when he caught a glimpse of a horse running loose, and, around a bend, he saw, right in front of him, what seemed to be its rider, lying on the path. He quickly dismounted to see if he could help, tied his horse to a tree and bent over the prone figure. At that moment, six mounted knights burst out of the forest and surrounded him! They leapt off their horses, saying nothing at all, and before he could reach his sword, they had wound a rope tightly around his arms.

Perhaps they thought it would be easy to subdue a man armed only for hunting. If so, they completely misjudged their quarry. There was no way to fasten the rope before Lancelot had thrust it aside and hurled himself toward them as if he were in combat armor. In his frenzy he seemed capable of breaking out of their circle, and they were more than a little impeded by their eagerness to take him alive. But fearing to lose him altogether, they brought him down with a sword thrust deep into his left shoulder, and he fainted from shock and pain. They tossed him onto his horse's back and led him away; he was fortunate to be spared awareness of the journey.

Hours later, he found himself in bed in an elegant room, feeling strangely at peace. His shoulder was heavily bandaged, and only vaguely could he remember what had happened to him. A woman was sitting beside him. Her air of agelessness, her beauty, the care he saw written in her eyes, all brought to mind the Lady of the Lake. She told him, however, that she was Morgan the Fay, and that some of her knights had found him roped and bound to his horse. They had scattered a band of would-be abductors and brought him to her castle. Her doctors had seen to his wound, and had insisted that he must have complete rest for a few days or he might lose the use of his arm. He would feel very weak, since he had bled profusely.

"I am most happy to offer hospitality to so distinguished a guest," she said. "I know that you are Lancelot of the Lake."

The knight recalled how he had gone out hunting and been attacked by armed men when he was defenseless. The thought of such a trap made him so furious that his face turned crimson and he began struggling to get up. Morgan put a cool hand on his forehead and begged him not to undo the doctors' good work. "My men said that those who attacked you did not escape unharmed, and whoever sent them will not be pleased with their work! They would have been hunted down and brought to justice, but it was more important to bring you quickly to a place where you could be taken care of."

"I apologize, my lady," said Lancelot. "I have not yet thanked you for your kindness. And I must ask you to do me a further service. Would you send someone to tell King Arthur and my friends at his court that I am safe with you? They must be worried that I am not back from the hunt."

"My messenger is already on his way," she claimed.

ℂ It was a long time before Lancelot's companions realized that he was missing. When the hunting ended in the late afternoon, the knights returned to the castle in small groups. Those who had been with Lancelot early in the day had seen him galloping off by himself, and they supposed he was late returning because he had gone further than anyone else. Galehaut, however, was already anxious, and when night came he could not conceal his agitation. Surely his friend must have met with an accident! It would be like him to try to bring down a boar all by himself! But nothing could be done until morning.

At first light, search parties fanned out through the forest. They rode all day long, carrying hunting horns with which to signal each other, but the horns were never put to use. Galehaut returned late in the evening, unable to speak to anyone, so overwhelming was his anguish. He spent little time in the great hall, where the absence of Lancelot and speculations about his fate were the only possible topics of conversation. Arthur was there, despondent; the queen had long since retired to her apartments. She felt that she wanted to die and yet could not bring herself to believe that anything had happened to Lancelot. The days wore on with no news, and gradually the searches were abandoned.

Galehaut, however, set out again with Lionel. They stopped at every dwelling place within a day's ride, at monasteries, manor houses, castles, where Lancelot could have found help had he been injured. Morgan's castle, however, made invisible by walls of mist, was thereby shielded from unwelcome visitors, just as ordinary castles were protected by moat and drawbridge. So Galehaut's quest led to nothing. He did not return to Carduel, but wandered on with less and less hope. His old illness came over him, and he ate almost nothing. Lionel became alarmed, seeing how weak Galehaut was becoming. He thought that perhaps at home in Sorelais he would feel better, and persuaded him that Lancelot might have gone there.

℃ Behind the enchanted walls, Lancelot's condition appeared to improve rapidly, although it would still be some time before he could ride. Morgan made him very comfortable, charming him with her delicate attentions. It was hard to reconcile such solicitude with the tales of her sorcery. He remembered having heard ill of her, but what he had learned about her hatred of Guenevere was now washed from memory by drugs and, grateful to her as he felt, he could not doubt her good will. Nor did it occur to him to wonder how she knew so much about his life.

In fact, that knowledge required no magical source. One of the attendants to the false Guenevere was in Morgan's service. She had given a detailed account of Lancelot's part in the trial and the intensity of his emotions regarding the queen; it was her opinion that Guenevere shared his feelings.

One afternoon, when Lancelot was well enough to walk slowly through the castle garden, Morgan said a few words about the queen. Lancelot had been surprised not to have heard from Guenevere, and Morgan's words were like a balm. "I don't go to court very often," she said. "My brother seems less fond of me than he was when we were children, although he has never given me a reason. I have wondered if it couldn't have been a simple misunderstanding. But I have always found the queen to be graciousness itself. Her beauty is a blessing to all who see her, and her voice the most enchanting I have ever heard. She reminds me of those mystical queens of legend whose very presence worked a kind of magic, for whom countless young men were willing to risk their lives."

"It's true; there is nothing the queen could ever ask that I would not gladly do."

They spoke then of inconsequential things until Lancelot went to his room to rest for a while. Feeling surprisingly tired, he stretched out on his comfortable bed and almost instantly fell asleep. *In the great hall in Carduel – or is it Camelot? – the king is dining in the company of his knights. The queen is absent. Someone says she is not feeling well. He is suddenly at her door, enters the chamber, and sees her, his peerless lady, laughing as she embraces a knight he does not recognize. He sees him undo the clasp at the neck of her cloak, reaching underneath.... In a moment he dreams he is on his way to the stables in Morgan's castle. He orders a groom to saddle his horse; there is no pain in his shoulder as he mounts and gallops away. The horse's hooves are silent on the cobblestones; the gate opens wide as he approaches. Then he is riding out into the forest –* and there, suddenly, he awoke, bewildered, unable to account for where he was or why he felt such a terrible despair. Then he remembered. The queen, his peerless lady, was laughing in the arms of another man.... With a raging cry, Lancelot fled, unable to outrun his anguish no matter how fast he went, unable to see for the tears that streamed down his face. He imagined himself confronting her, but the thought was unbearable; he felt he might kill her sooner than let her speak. Not for one instant did he doubt the truth of what he had seen. He rode all night long, and, in the morning, found himself on the way to Sorelais.

ℭ Galehaut had already been at home for some time. Deeply troubled to have found no trace of Lancelot, he had asked Lionel to return to Arthur's court in case there was news – not that he harbored more than the faintest hope. The lordly castle of Sorham, once his pride, was visibly crumbling, and his confidence was falling away with it. Lionel consented to Galehaut's request only on condition that he place himself in the care of the monks in the monastery near Tessaline; they were known to be skilled at healing. He agreed, and the two men departed from the castle, each following his own path.

Alarmed by Galehaut's emaciated appearance, and even more by the sadness which he tried to conceal, the monks put him to bed in a sun-filled chamber and brought him soothing potions made from the herbs and simples of their garden. They did their best to persuade him to take some nourishment. But his ignorance of Lancelot's fate was devastating – worse, surely, than any reliable knowledge might be, so that the monks' ministrations met with a resistance that, although unwilled, was stubborn. With time, though, their patient began to yield, even daring to hope for some positive word from Lionel; perhaps Lancelot had returned to court! It was bittersweet to remember how his companion had been with him in this very place. Surely they would be together again some day, here or elsewhere! Gradually, the calm presence of the monks and the serene regularity of their chanting encouraged Galehaut to think about himself, about the short time that remained to him, and about the works he had yet to perform. He knew that he would need strength to carry out the program he had set for his final years, and he resolved to do all he could to improve his health.

Sooner than the monks considered prudent, however, Galehaut set out on a journey around his kingdom, to do good works among the poor, and to arrange for churches to be built where they were needed. Everywhere he looked for young men of promise who could not afford the equipment of a knight, and he provided them with armor and good horses. His people had always loved him for his splendor and the glory of his conquests, but now they began to revere him for his kindness. There was some comfort for him in this, and in the hope that what he was doing would help redeem the excesses that had marked his early years. Yet he would have abandoned his travels in an instant had he learned that Lancelot was on his way to Sorham.

℘ It was fortunate that the guards at the causeway over the Severn recognized Lancelot, since he was in no condition to fight for permission to cross. He was given a warm welcome, but when they saw how weakened he was by the wound, which had not healed properly, they refused to allow him to continue his journey on horseback. The knight had no strength to protest. They organized a litter and sent a rider ahead to let the people at Sorham know that they were coming, asking them to send for Galehaut's most skillful doctor. Although they traveled in easy stages, Lancelot grew increasingly fatigued and his injured shoulder ever more painful. His mood, however, was lightened by the expectation of an imminent reunion with his companion.

For the duration of his absence, Galehaut had entrusted the city of Sorham to his noble vassal, Bademagus, and it was he who had the gates of the castle thrown open to greet the visitor. Lancelot was alarmed to find Galehaut absent, nor could the sight of a ruined watchtower and the deeply fissured walls give him much comfort. Bademagus's reassurances failed to prove convincing, especially as he admitted that Galehaut had been ill and depressed following his fruitless search for Lancelot. The young knight understood that Galehaut was not simply doing good works. He was preparing for his death.

"My lord," he appealed to Bademagus, "we must call him back to Sorham! I wish I could ride after him myself! But now we'll have to trust to messengers."

Bademagus agreed immediately. Lancelot then allowed himself to be put to bed and endure the doctor's attentions. He rebandaged the shoulder and told Lancelot that if he did not rest long enough for his wound to heal properly, his very life would be at risk.

That night Lancelot lay restless, drifting in and out of sleep, but, in either state, agitated by thoughts of the queen and especially by terrible premonitions of Galehaut's fate. He had never forgotten Master Elias's warning that he, Lancelot, would be the instrument of his companion's death, and now, in some

way he could not understand, it seemed the prophecy was
nearing its fulfillment.

As the night wore on, anxiety turned to frantic despera-
tion, until Lancelot, heedless of his condition, jumped out of
bed and hastily threw on clothes that he could barely see in
the smoky light of his single taper. He would somehow, and
faster than any messenger, find Galehaut himself! He was
growing feverish. He could neither feel nor, in the dim light,
see how his movements opened the shoulder wound once
more and renewed the bleeding. He found his way to the door,
rushed out, almost fell down the narrow, uneven steps that
led to the ground floor, remembered the castle well enough
to locate the kitchen exit and, after that, the little postern gate
which, now barely hinged and certainly no longer locked,
offered him a way out beyond the fortress walls. He thought
he was on his way to the stables, but realized after a while that
he had gone in the wrong direction. Never mind! He would
run. In his confusion, with nothing to guide him through the
darkness, he strayed from the rutted path and stumbled into
a maze of forest underbrush. He fell; he picked himself up; he
ran – downward, it seemed; he slipped again, collapsed, and
rolled a short way to the edge of a lake. He lay still.

A hermit found him in the morning, barely conscious,
incoherent and badly hurt. The holy man realized that he must
have come from the castle but could hardly return there in
his present state; nor could he be left alone while help was
sought. Removing the most muddy, blood-soaked parts of

Lancelot's bandages and clothing, useless for the moment, he simply left them on the ground, intending to recover them once he had attended to their owner. His hut was close by, hidden from view by thick foliage and the rocky hillside, and there he managed to lead the knight.

℘ One of the riders dispatched by Bademagus found Galehaut in the most distant town of the kingdom, and the message sent him galloping frantically back toward Sorham. Although there had been few details, it was apparent that Lancelot's condition was serious enough to prevent his seeking Galehaut himself. The older man was troubled by what this failure might foretell, but his anxiety was overwhelmed by the joy of knowing that Lancelot was alive, in Sorelais, and that he would see him soon. The days of his hurried ride back to Sorham passed in a blur of excited expectation.

It was not Lancelot, however, who welcomed him across the lowered drawbridge, but a muted and evasive Bademagus. Faces along the way were drawn and unsmiling; eyes turned away from his glance. In moments Galehaut went from puzzlement to suspicion and from suspicion to anguish. "Where is Lancelot?" he cried out at last, "and why has no one yet uttered his name?"

Then, to his horror, Galehaut learned what there was to know: his companion's disappearance during the night, blood stains on his bedding and on the floor, indeed a whole trail of blood leading wildly along a rough path in the forest and then down to the shore of Sorham Lake. And the blood-soaked garments. And no further trace. It seemed all too clear that Lancelot was dead.

Galehaut insisted on going to the lake, although it had rained and there could be nothing to see. He fell on the ground at the water's edge and wept. Then he lay silently, without moving, for a long time. So this was how Lancelot was meant to bring about his death, darkness bringing on more darkness. Would they meet beyond this world? It was the only hope that Galehaut had left. As night was coming on, Bademagus knelt down beside his liege lord and begged him to return home. Galehaut, still silent, rose heavily to his feet and mounted his horse. At the castle, he spoke to no one but went directly to his chamber. Servants who came to offer food were turned away.

In the morning it seemed he had not stirred all night. "How is it with you, my lord?" asked a man who had been with him for many years. There was no response. The servant sent word to Bademagus, who needed no more than a glance to know the truth. The sorrow engraved on Galehaut's noble face would be there forever. He called together the members of the household to tell them that the Lord of the Distant Isles was dead.

℄ Under the hermit's care, Lancelot recovered his wits and began to recover his strength, despite the loss of blood, although the repeated tearing open of the wound in his shoulder made it slow to heal. The hermit was impressed by

the young man's beauty, even in his present state and with all his battle scars, and wondered what could account for his evident unhappiness. Lancelot responded with courteous thanks to the holy man's solicitude, but seemed not to care if he lived or died. In fact, he could not imagine how his life would go on. He had long thought of himself as Queen Guenevere's knight and as Galehaut's companion. These were the bonds, above all others, that had given him, as an adult, a sense of who he was and where he stood in life. Now he was convinced that Guenevere had deceived him, and because of him, Galehaut was facing death! These ties, which had defined his very self, were being cruelly cut. He felt cast adrift and utterly forlorn.

One morning, the hermit came to his bedside to tell him, with discreet excitement, that a beautiful lady of the noblest bearing had arrived to visit him. She had come accompanied by a single handmaiden and was waiting for him under the oak just outside the hermitage. Lancelot felt his heart leap, and he stood up with a flush of expectancy. He did not wonder who had found her way to his retreat.

She greeted him as she had often done. Then, "My prince," she said, "I have come to you with sad news." She paused only long enough to embrace him, the young man whom she had shaped for whatever purpose of her own but whom she had always cherished with a love as great as any natural mother's.

"Your companion returned to the castle of Sorham only to be confronted with signs that you had died. A trail of blood ending at the water's edge and a pile of blood-stained cloth seemed to leave no doubt. I don't need to describe to you what immense grief this illusion brought to Galehaut. Without you, there was nothing left for him in life. He turned his face toward the wall that night and never wakened from his sleep."

Lancelot's heartbreaking intuition was thus confirmed. No news could have brought him greater sorrow or more readily released the tears that now ran down his cheeks in silent mourning. Had it truly been inevitable that Galehaut's love for him and his for Galehaut would reach this end? Nothing was less certain, and yet he felt no surprise. Perhaps if he had long ago turned away from the queen. . . . Now she had turned away from him, but this recent separation could hardly have saved the life of his companion. He was overcome by a heavy sadness that rent his soul. Unlike his response to other griefs, this time there were no loud cries and frenzy. He had loved Galehaut for his magnanimity, for the great heart that ruled his thoughts and deeds – and for his love. He lamented the loss with a quiet despair worthy of his friend.

"To think," he said after some time had passed, "had it not been for the kindness of the hermit, no one would have imagined I had drowned, and Galehaut would not have been killed by a misunderstanding. The hermit told me that when he returned to look for my clothes, they were gone."

"Had it not been for the kindness of the hermit," she answered, "you yourself would have died. For Galehaut the result would very soon have been the same. The workings of true prophecies are beyond our understanding. They shift and reshape themselves, and their details elude our grasp even as we watch them gradually come true." But Lancelot was not ready for such abstractions; they offered him little comfort.

The Lady of the Lake knew, as Lancelot could but dimly sense, that the young man's pain was all the sharper for having no precedent in his experience. No more than shadowy memories had been left by the loss of his parents, and though he had seen, and caused, countless deaths in knightly combat, only now had a tie to someone dear to him been severed. The reality of death had, in truth, been hidden from him. With the loss of Galehaut, his youth came to an end, and with it passed a love that could never be replaced.

"But one day you will be reunited with your companion," the Lady added. "It will be in death, and so it will be forever. Meanwhile, you will bear him in your heart and that will be a consolation."

Lancelot would have gladly ended all conversation at this point, although it would only have deepened his distress to see the Lady of the Lake depart. She, however, had a measured time for her visit and knew it was necessary to speak about the queen. "Morgan the Fay has done her – and you – a great injustice. It is not a secret that she has detested Guenevere ever since her brother Arthur chose the most beautiful of women for his wife. Morgan felt displaced and bitter. She has never forgiven Arthur, and she considers Guenevere an enemy whose life she must somehow bring to ruin. You are aware of her vile attempt to replace the queen with her half-sister. When, thanks to your defense, that plan failed, she conceived another strategy: as soon as she could be sure of the bond between you and Guenevere, she would use you as a tool to undo the queen's happiness. Do not think that Morgan's men rescued you from abductors. Her men – "

And Lancelot had no trouble completing the sentence: "– were my abductors! And the dream in which I learned of Guenevere's infidelity to me – "

"– was a falsehood produced by enchantment. Morgan's sorcery both induced the dream and convinced you to believe its tale. It didn't matter what searing effects it might have on you, as long as it provoked a brutal rupture with the queen."

Alongside the overwhelming sorrow caused by Galehaut's death and the weight he felt at having been instrumental in the event, Lancelot now found himself assailed by shame. How could he have let himself be so duped by Morgan as to doubt – indeed, deny – the truth of the queen's love? He had let their bond be severed without a moment's hesitation, without the slightest questioning. Such had been the potency of Morgan's spell, but such had also been his innocence – and his lack of trust. He would be wary of accepting such appearances in the future.

But for all his distress, Lancelot was also stirred by the joyous thought that he could see the queen again and that she would not turn him away. This was, in fact, the final message that the Lady of the Lake had come to convey. Soon it would be time to return to King Arthur's court, to the Round Table, and to Queen Guenevere's affections.

Now, however, he must attend to the burial of Galehaut. Lancelot thanked the hermit for his unstinting care and, with the Lady of the Lake, went back to the castle at Sorham, where he was greeted with astonishment, as if returned from the dead. His emotion rendered him all but speechless, and so the Lady of the Lake related to Bademagus how the hermit had rescued him and had unwittingly let it appear that he had drowned. Lancelot found his companion laid out in the same chapel where Master Elias had once spoken with him of life and death. From that moment, right through the night, he kept a solitary vigil over the body, none of the people of the castle daring to disturb his tears and contemplation.

In the morning, before mass, the Lady of the Lake gave Lancelot one final motherly embrace, and departed.

❡ None of the barons of Sorelais disputed the young knight's wish to bury their liege lord as he saw fit. Even once it was clear that he would thus be laid to rest outside his own kingdom, they all agreed that Galehaut's final place would most properly be with his companion. And so a solemn procession of knights set out with Lancelot from Sorham slowly bearing the body of Galehaut, pulled by four tall black horses, through the villages and forests of the land, past the Severn, across all the leagues to Joyous Guard.

There, in the fortress that Lancelot had once freed from its terrifying enchantments and made his own, the castle whose name had thereby changed from Dolorous to Joyous but which was now filled with sadness once again, Lancelot ordered that a magnificent tomb be built. It was crafted not of wood nor even gold or silver but entirely of precious stones; these were cut and joined and set in porphyry with a subtle art that barely seemed the work of mortal men. It was placed in the castle cemetery where Lancelot had, some years before, discovered the grave intended for himself. To that site beside his own, six vassals bore Galehaut dressed in full armor, and Lancelot himself, trembling and in tears, laid to rest the body of his companion. He kissed him three times on the lips in such agony that his heart came close to breaking. Then he covered him with a pall of richest silk brocade and lowered the stone lid. It bore, for all to see, the inscription:

HERE LIES GALEHAUT,
THE SON OF THE GIANTESS,
LORD OF THE DISTANT ISLES,
WHO DIED FOR THE LOVE
OF LANCELOT

BOOK ELEVEN + THE DEATH OF LANCELOT

THE LANCELOT WHO RETURNED TO Camelot some months later was not so much changed in appearance as in his very being. He had stayed at Joyous Guard in solitude, remembering all that he and Galehaut had been to each other, from the day they met on the battlefield when the Lord of the Distant Isles had put himself at the service of the Black Knight, to the last time he saw Galehaut alive. At that final encounter, with a semblance of cheer, his companion had wished him good hunting, and Lancelot realized that Galehaut had not accompanied him that day because the hunt was to celebrate Lancelot's return to the Round Table. In truth, he had had no desire to bind himself to King Arthur, except that it was the preference of the queen. Even Galehaut acknowledged that he could not refuse her.

Over and over again he relived the moment when Galehaut went to King Arthur and surrendered, although he had been on the point of conquering his kingdom. Lancelot had felt then, and continued to feel now, unworthy of such a selfless commitment to love. He knew that never again would he find in this world a man of Galehaut's quality.

He thought also about the queen, how he would never have dared approach her had not Galehaut's generosity made it possible. That had been like a gift of life itself, a pure and unshadowed joy. Yet now, perhaps because so much that he depended on had been lost, including, for a time, his trust in Guenevere, his longing for her was marked by a reluctance, by a painful new awareness of the king.

He could not know what life had been like for her since the day of that unlucky hunt. Apart from the Lady of Malehaut there was no one in whom she could confide, and once the search for Lancelot had been abandoned, there was very little to say. Lancelot's disappearance had occurred without a witness; Lionel had reported Galehaut's presence in Sorelais but knew nothing further of him or Lancelot. Guenevere would have preferred to remain in seclusion, but knew that would cause too much comment. Once again she appeared in the great hall, trying to bring comfort to those around her, especially to Arthur who feared for his kingdom. In the terrible isolation of her perplexity and grief, she felt at a great distance from him and the entire court. Even to learn the worst would be better, she felt, than to dwell in uncertainty; it was terrible to think that nothing might ever be known. Her hope was fading away.

By the time a courier arrived from Joyous Guard, she could barely comprehend that he was announcing Lancelot. She had waited for him so long that, at first, she was more vexed than relieved; but when she saw him standing before the assembled court, her joy was so intense she almost fainted. She could barely grasp what he was reporting. He spoke of Galehaut's death. Only for himself was that news of supreme importance. Everyone else was so glad to have Lancelot back, they could think of little else.

Lancelot's solace was the queen. She had touched his heart the first moment he saw her, and all his knightly prowess, all the renown he had sought and gained, had been inspired by his love for her. Galehaut had understood this and sacrificed himself in love as in warfare, yielding to Guenevere as he had yielded to Arthur. Lancelot realized, perhaps for the first time, the inestimable value of what he had lost. But even in his sorrow, he longed for the queen.

℄ The lovers had only once before been alone together, but now their meetings became increasingly frequent, and they lived for nothing else. Lancelot had often to absent himself from court, sometimes alone, sometimes with other knights, to ensure the safety of King Arthur's realm. Thanks to his prowess and steadfast allegiance, threats from without were repelled and justice maintained within. He shone as brightly as ever in tournaments and wars – admired, loved, and feared. The king relied on his commitment and his valor with grateful assurance, and Lancelot never failed to satisfy, and even to surpass, his hopes. But in truth it was always the queen for whom he battled and who guided his behavior in combat as at court. Even at the age of fifty, she was the most beautiful woman he had ever seen. Everything he undertook, he undertook for her, and he gloried in her approval. With Galehaut gone, he could convince himself that the queen was both lover and companion, even as the absence of his irreplaceable friend cast a shadow over his joy. Guenevere thrived on Lancelot's adoration, imagining her marriage and her love as complementary rather than conflicting. They both tried to remain absolutely discreet, yet inevitably, in the course of time, traces of their sentiments became noticeable.

They were unaware that one day Morgan asked the king to receive her in private, claiming to have information that touched his honor. Arthur knew that his sister would go to any lengths to discredit Guenevere; she had already proved as much. Still, he let her convince him to have the queen watched. He selected the knight named Agravain for the purpose, swearing him to secrecy. Agravain would be more inclined than most to accept such a task, for he was known to be jealous of Lancelot on behalf of his brother Gawain, now only the second most renowned of Arthur's warriors. Not that Gawain himself had ever felt uncomfortably displaced by the newer hero, but his younger brother resented the dimming of his own, reflected, glory.

One evening Agravain saw the queen leave the great hall at Camelot rather early. He slipped out after her. The night was not too dark for him to see Guenevere cross the garden and walk rapidly toward a pavilion sometimes used for guests. Half an hour later, Lancelot followed. Although it was clear that he was unarmed, Agravain went to the watch tower and returned with four other knights. For all the lovers' intentness on each other, the sound of footsteps and the clanking of metal outside the pavilion made it clear that their tryst was not a secret. Lancelot, enraged rather than alarmed, was sure he could save them both, but the queen thought that an attempt to escape with him would make her guilt even more apparent. "As long as you are safe, they won't dare to touch me, for fear of what you would do!" He seized an axe that was hanging on the wall, and abruptly opened the door. The man who was leaning against it lost his balance and fell victim to the blade. Lancelot kicked the door closed and seized the intruder's sword and shield. Then, flinging the door wide open, he fought his way past the others, leaving two men dead behind him. He leapt onto a horse that stood nearby and galloped away. Agravain forced Guenevere to accompany him to the king.

Arthur had never wanted to believe the rumors about Lancelot and the queen. For him, Lancelot had been the very model of valor and loyalty. The queen he had always loved with adoration, despite the passing charms of other women. So he had stubbornly gone on trusting in her innocence. This time, however, he had to face not a rumor, but a reality. He turned from Guenevere in revulsion, convinced at last of a betrayal that could have only one outcome. His wife's treachery called for the ultimate punishment. Arthur ordered a guard to lock her in her chambers until he could have her put to death. All that mattered was revenge – and the need to act quickly, before Lancelot could intervene.

Just one of Arthur's liege men dared to object. Should the queen be killed, Gawain told his uncle in a tone that admitted of no doubt, he would leave the court forever, ally himself with Lancelot and destroy the Round Table. "What the queen has done is far less a sin than murder! She has always been the glory of this kingdom, and deserves our compassion now. Let her live out her days in peace. Remove her to a holy place where she can pray for her sins."

At last, for fear that Gawain would carry out his threat, the king agreed to this plan. The Lady of Malehaut would accompany Guenevere to a suitable convent, and the two women were sent on their way the very next morning. Arthur would never see the queen again.

℣ From a distance, Lancelot watched as Guenevere and her escort rode away. His almost irresistible impulse was to hurl himself upon them, to fight his way through to her. Galehaut had once imagined carrying her off to Sorelais, an idea they had rejected as completely unacceptable. But now he had no refuge to offer her, much less a kingdom, and, more keenly than ever before, he felt the loss of his inheritance. Too late now to recapture Benoic! All he had to call his own was the fortress, Joyous Guard, but that was within King Arthur's lands and would surely be attacked. In any event, Guenevere would be an outlaw. The king would never give up pursuing them, and were she to be captured she would no doubt be burned at the stake. And as she herself had refused to come away with him when they were discovered together, there was no reason to think she would change her mind. She could not deny her guilt any more than he could; the king would never forgive her, even if contrition were to win her the mercy of God.

It was hard for him to imagine such redemption for himself. His love was lost to him, and that he, unlike the queen, still had his freedom could only be justified by taking vengeance on the spy. When all that remained of Guenevere was a faint cloud of dust on the road, Lancelot spurred his horse and galloped to Camelot, over the drawbridge and straight into the courtyard of the castle. At the top of his lungs, he shouted out a challenge to Agravain. The response was immediate. Although Gawain tried desperately to prevent him, Agravain rode out to confront a knight against whom he had little chance of prevailing. He had assumed that Lancelot would be captured with the queen, but he and his men had failed. And when he thought of those killed, he felt he was shamed forever should he not try to avenge them.

The duel was very brief. As the horses drove straight toward each other, Agravain's lance splintered on Lancelot's shield, even as a blow powerful enough to split an oak sent him flying, dead, to the ground.

❡ Gawain had felt like a sleeper trapped in a nightmare, unable to intervene, paralyzed with horror. Standing over his brother Agravain's body, with the king and knights of the Round

Table looking on, all of them as powerless as he was, Gawain knew that his world, the world in which the mission of knights was to protect the weak and defend the right, had come to an end. The greatest knight ever seen, the man he had admired above all others and to whom the very kingdom owed its continued existence, that knight he was now bound to try and destroy. If only such a friend had not taken his brother's life!

To defend the right – but there was nothing here that was right: the peerless queen disgraced, yes; and if Lancelot had not championed her against the false queen, she would have been put to death by Arthur's command. His brother turned spy, but for jealousy of Lancelot, as Gawain knew very well, not from any principle. Guenevere had had no trial. And if there had been one, would she not have accused the king of a faithlessness known to all? Would she not have reminded him of how he had insisted she persuade Lancelot to stay at court? Even now, Lancelot could ride away – no one would have dared to stop him – but he waited there, honor-bound, immobile on his horse, and Gawain heard himself say what his friend was expecting to hear: that the death of Agravain would cost Lancelot his life, or Gawain would lose his own.

Lancelot too felt controlled by forces set in motion long ago, but now so potent they could no longer be denied. Gawain had befriended him when he first came to court. And he was, next to Galehaut, the knight whom Lancelot had found most admirable. Moreover, he was the queen's nephew, as devoted to her as she was to him. What would she want Lancelot to do? Could he simply refuse to respond to Gawain's challenge? He had no fear of being called a coward, but he would have to answer for Agravain's death; simply to leave would only put off an inevitable confrontation. He thought ruefully that his shoulder wound, never entirely healed, would give his opponent an advantage, assuming that Gawain himself had been restored to health.

Gawain, now fully armed and riding a fresh horse, appeared on the field; the herald signaled the onset of the combat. Their first pass unhorsed them both, so perfect was their skill, and they stood, facing each other, with drawn swords. They could have said something, then, of what was in their hearts, but there seemed to be no words. They fought with immense sadness, as if moving through water. Gawain's strength, as always, increased when the sun was at its height; after that, Lancelot began to prevail. The hours went by. The ground where they fought was covered with chainmail links and pieces of shields; blood was running from Gawain's nose and mouth, as well as from countless wounds. Lancelot was only slightly better off. Any other knights in the world would have given up or died long since, but through the afternoon these two showed no signs of fatigue or pain.

When the light began to fade, however, Gawain had scarcely the strength to hold his sword; everyone could see that his defeat was certain. He paused for a moment to take a breath, and Lancelot said, "My lord, a knight accused of unlawful killing must fight in his own defense, but only until vespers. I think you could now agree that I've answered your challenge. I am ready to continue, if you insist, but one of us will not survive."

"Then one of us will not survive."

Lancelot was pained to hear this, almost preferring to die himself rather than kill so valiant a knight. He turned to King Arthur: "My lord, I have asked Sir Gawain to put an end to this duel lest one of us come to harm."

The king knew very well what the outcome of further combat would be, and grateful for Lancelot's generosity, he replied, "Gawain is not obliged to declare the battle over, but you have my permission to withdraw, if that is your wish. His challenge has been well and truly answered."

"My lord, if I thought it would not be held against me, I would leave the field to Sir Gawain."

"I am glad to have it so."

"Then I will take my leave, with your permission."

"And may God protect you."

Lancelot stood still until his horse was led onto the field. Then he mounted and in the gathering darkness rode away toward Joyous Guard.

For a few moments no one moved; they listened in silence to the receding footfalls of Lancelot's horse. Its pace was slow. The knights of the Round Table knew that they had witnessed

that day a magnificence of valor not to be seen again. The glory
of King Arthur's court depended on Lancelot. Now, with Sir
Gawain almost certainly close to death, the kingdom would
be vulnerable as never before.

King Arthur bent over the grievously wounded knight and
gave way to his sorrow. "Fortune that has favored me for so
long now casts me down! Dear nephew, please try to live – you
are all I have left!"

Gawain was placed carefully on a litter and carried to his
lodgings, where doctors did what they could to make him
comfortable. Precious ointments were spread over his wounds,
and bandages were wrapped tightly around them. Soothing
potions were brought to ease his pain, but he was unable to
swallow. He lay in a restless torpor, barely conscious.

℧ Days went by with no change, then weeks. Camelot, always
so full of activity, was silent as never before. No knights were
starting out or returning from adventures; in the evenings,
no minstrel sang. The arrival of a messenger one morning
was at first a welcome diversion, but the news he brought was
grim. King Arthur's bastard son Mordred, a result of the king's
youthful infatuation with his half-sister Morgause, had seldom
been seen at court. He had never won any favor with his
father, who greatly preferred his eldest nephew and, more
recently, the son of Ban. The more Gawain and Lancelot
attracted the world's admiration, the more virulent and hos-
tile Mordred became, and his hatred was always focused on

the king. Over the years, Mordred had made alliances with powerful Saxon lords, promising that they would one day hold the lands of Arthur's kingdom.

News of the sad events in Camelot did not fail to reach him promptly, and he rejoiced to think that his moment was finally at hand. He assembled a vast army across the frontier, and had already moved into Logres when his ultimatum was brought to Arthur: "Welcome me as your overlord, or your kingdom and your life will be forfeit."

Before responding, Arthur went to visit Gawain who said, "My lord, I implore you not to fight with Mordred! Close to death as I am, some things have been shown to me. You may indeed kill your son, but I know he'll have inflicted on you a wound you will not survive."

"But I cannot simply stay here and let him invade us! What honor would I have left if I were seen to be afraid? If I bring an army against him there is some hope, however slight. If I don't, I will even more surely find death at his hands."

"There is one thing you can do, and I beg you, if ever you have loved me, to do it. You must send for Lancelot."

Arthur was astonished to hear Gawain offer such advice, but, although he admired him for it, he felt obliged to reply, "I cannot bring myself to ask for his help."

"When I die," said Gawain, already on another plane of thought, "please let him know that I thought of him at the last, and thought of him as the man I most loved and esteemed in my life, both for his prowess and his perfect courtesy." Gawain said no more, but closed his eyes and lay still. He seemed to have fallen unconscious, but Arthur could not bear to leave him. After a time, he heard Gawain whisper, "God, judge me not according to my sins." Then the sound of his labored breathing came to an end.

That night the king kept vigil over his nephew. He looked much older when he appeared next day in the great hall and ordered that Gawain receive every possible honor and be laid to rest, as he had requested, beside his brother. The king himself placed over the body a cloth stiff with gold and heavy with jewels. The procession that set out for Gawain's homeland consisted only of priests and squires; every knight was commanded to prepare himself for war.

℃ There was at Salisbury Plain a large rock on which Merlin the sorcerer had inscribed a prophecy:

ON THIS PLAIN THERE WILL BE A BATTLE AFTER WHICH THE KINGDOM OF LOGRES WILL BE ORPHANED FOREVER.

Even as King Arthur looked at this, Mordred's army began to darken the horizon. Soon he realized that it was at least twice the size of his own. Only seventy-two knights of the Round Table were with him, and he sadly thought of Lancelot, who would surely have come to help him, had he been asked. Assuming a confidence that he did not feel, he organized ten battalions, the first to be commanded by Sir Yvain, the second by King Yon, the last by himself, exhorting them all to win honor for themselves and their king. Mordred was on the march with twenty battalions, the first two entirely made up of Saxons, whose hatred of Arthur was such that they made up in ferocity for their lesser skill at fighting. Others came from Scotland, Ireland, and Wales. Now they could see King Arthur's banners fluttering in the wind, where his men waited immobile on their horses; and now they came closer still, and a thousand lances were lowered as one. The armies came together with a sound louder than ten claps of thunder. Yvain rode against Arcans, the Saxon king's nephew, and cut him down. But the triumph was short.

The Saxon king tried to avenge his nephew's death, but Yvain sent him, headless, to his own death, and the Saxon battalions fled as the Britons kept cutting them down from behind. But the Irish came to their help, strong, well-rested fighters who inflicted such wounds on the Britons that all of them would have been lost had King Yon not led his men into the melee. Finding Yvain on foot, badly wounded, and surrounded by enemies, King Yon scattered them with such speed and fury that Yvain could be mounted again. They both resumed fighting, but an Irish warrior hurled himself at King Yon and took his life. Yvain's vengeance was swift, but brought no satisfaction: "If only your death could bring that great king back!" he sighed.

The ground was covered with dead and wounded knights;

frenzied horses galloped everywhere, with no one to stop them. So many valiant men were killed on that day that not only the kingdom of Logres, but many other lands as well were left to the mercy of marauders. The world would never again hold such a wealth of brave and worthy leaders.

Arthur looked around him on the field. Ten thousand men – foot-soldiers and knights – had come there to fight; now only six hundred were left, and with them only four of the Round Table knights. Then he saw Mordred ride against Yvain and, with a single blow, cut him down. The king's heart nearly failed him; but Mordred came galloping in his direction, and his strength returned to him in an all-consuming rage. Both lances were shattered in the shock of their encounter, but neither man was unhorsed.

As Arthur unsheathed Excalibur, light flashed from its jeweled hilt. Raising his sword with both hands, the king brought it crashing down on his son's head, but before the blow fell, Mordred's sword had pierced his father's hauberk and plunged deep into his chest. Excalibur cracked Mordred's helmeted skull as easily as an eggshell. He fell onto his horse's neck and, tangled in the reins, was carried, dead, back toward his own lines. Arthur, mortally wounded, slipped to the ground. His remaining men, wild with fury, chased the retreating Saxons, who turned around and fought on. By evening, only King Arthur and one knight, a young man named Girflet, were still alive – and the king was dying.

After a night spent in prayer, King Arthur asked Girflet to take Excalibur and ride to a nearby lake. He was to throw the sword into the water.

"But my lord! How can I destroy so marvelous a weapon? If you have no further use for it, give it to me!"

"Do you think that well of yourself? Only Lancelot is worthy of my sword, and to him I would bequeath it, if I could. Now go and do what I said."

When Girflet returned after a while, Arthur asked, "What did you see when you threw the sword into the lake?"

"Only the water closing over it, my lord."

The king had been lying, exhausted and growing weaker, under a tree. Now he sat up against the trunk, and the knight was awed by the majesty of his presence. "Do not lie to me! You have sworn to serve your king and to obey him. Do not presume to decide the destiny of the sword I have carried into battle all my life! Now go and do what I cannot do for myself."

Girflet hurried to where he had hidden Excalibur and hurled it as far as he could toward the center of the lake. But it did not fall directly into the water. It was grasped instead by the hand of a slender arm that had suddenly risen above the surface. Then arm and uplifted sword sank back into the water and disappeared.

Struck with wonder, Girflet ran back to King Arthur and reported what he had witnessed. "Thank you," said the king. "Now saddle the horses and ride with me to the sea."

When they reached the shore, the king, with great effort, dismounted and said, "I release you from my service, good friend. Leave me alone here, and know that you will never see me again."

"Where are you going, my lord?"

"That I cannot tell you."

Girflet rode away. There was a sudden rainstorm, and he took shelter beneath a tree on top of a hill. When the rain stopped, he looked back toward the king. A boat with fair silk sails appeared in the distance and stopped close to where Arthur lay on the ground. In it, Girflet recognized Morgan the Fay, standing at the prow. Arthur rose to his feet and, leading his horse, stepped lightly into the boat. Girflet caught a final glimpse of the king, lying with his head on Morgan's lap, as the boat headed into the mist that blurred the horizon.

℞ News of the King's death spread rapidly through his lands. At her convent Guenevere mourned the husband for whom she had always felt a profound affection. She had never forgotten the radiant young ruler who had chosen her as his bride.

The Lady of Malehaut said, "Alas, my lady! When King Uther Pendragon died, and King Arthur was still a child, even houses like this were not safe from the warring barons. Each one thought he could make the land his own by overpowering his neighbors. There was no safe asylum anywhere. King Arthur changed all that, and we have known the splendor of his reign. But now the situation is worse than at the very start, because the king has neither left a son nor designated an heir. Our world has reached its end."

"I know you blame me for that," said Guenevere, "and for Galehaut's death too, and indeed I blame myself, most bitterly. But the Lady of the Lake told me that my love, which the world considered folly and betrayal, was wisdom. Lancelot was the noblest and most valiant knight ever seen, and I was the occasion for his great deeds. He asked for no reward, only that I allow him to be my knight. He never knew what fear was except in my presence; I was the one to act on his unspoken, and perhaps unrecognized, desire.

"The king would have had me killed on the word of an impostor, had not Lancelot fought three knights to save me. Long before that, Galehaut would have conquered all of Logres, had Lancelot not intervened. Always Arthur feared that, were it not for Lancelot, his enemies would overwhelm him. He forced me to have Lancelot remain at court, when I knew that it would be wrong for him to do so. Many times Arthur betrayed me, and his loves endangered the realm. My love was its protection, although there was no way to save it in the end."

℺ When Lancelot reached Joyous Guard after his duel with Sir Gawain, his condition was alarming. Although the people of the castle were happy to have their liberator with them once again, they could sense it would not be for long. Doctors applied their arts with diligence, but weeks went by with no discernible improvement. They were discouraged by their patient's lack of vigor. He seemed to undergo their treatments without caring whether they were effective. Finally, they told Lancelot there was nothing more to be done.

Lionel, sometimes accompanied by his younger brother, Bors, never left his cousin's bedside, trying to make him comfortable and to cheer him. Indeed, the one subject that seemed to interest Lancelot was the ceremony he planned for Lionel's knighting. When it took place, he appeared in the great hall, looking somewhat like himself again. All the people of the castle were in attendance, as the young man knelt before his cousin, the son of King Ban of Benoic, who solemnly touched his shoulders with the sword that had once belonged to Galehaut. Then Lancelot, torn between regret and hope, entrusted the precious weapon to the new knight. There was a feast in Lionel's honor that evening, but Lancelot attended it with a heavy heart.

It was not long before a messenger arrived with a letter from the Lady of Malehaut, telling him that Guenevere had died, "not of any accident or illness. She just seemed to waste away, eating less and less, until she had no more strength. After the death of King Arthur, she had hoped you would come to her, although she knew how badly you were wounded in the battle with Gawain. The abbess of our convent, however, persuaded her to think of the salvation of her soul, and finally she decided to take the veil. I accompanied her in this, and will spend the rest of my life in this holy place. The queen was buried here, as no one knows what happened to the body of the king."

Lancelot fell into a restless lethargy from which nothing could rouse him. For him, the world was empty, with no more use for valor, and nothing left to inspire it. He wondered how Lionel and Bors would face the new times. He had not succeeded in winning his kingdom back from the usurper; would his cousins ever regain the land from which they, too, had been forced to flee? Galehaut had wanted to make all that possible, but he had declined his companion's help. Soon Arthur's kingdom would be fought over by the enemies on its borders; its glory would be only a fading memory. Had it not been for him, Galehaut would have ruled in Arthur's place; perhaps that would have been better. He could not imagine his life if he hadn't loved the queen, but had they not been discovered, he would have fought against Mordred with Arthur, if Mordred had dared to attack. The result might have been different. Or he might have died in battle, rather than linger here so wretchedly. He began to have high fevers; his old shoulder wound had become infected, causing him great pain. All he could do was lie in bed, waiting for the end. He asked to see a priest, but was more disturbed than ever after his visit.

One morning, on the tenth day before May, a servant told Lionel that a tall lady of great beauty was asking to see him. At the sight of the Lady of the Lake, Lionel felt a sudden happiness, as if everything could still be made right. But in his heart he knew why she had come. He answered her anxious questions, and then she went to Lancelot. He had been for days in a state between sleep and unconsciousness, tormented still by dreams and memories, but he opened his eyes and saw her. "My dear prince!" she said, embracing him. For a moment he came back to life, glad that she was there, but soon he collapsed in her arms. Neither of them moved for a long time. Then she began to sing a song which had often calmed him to sleep as a child, when he was over-tired from riding through the forest or from play.

"One more time," he murmured, just as he used to do, and, with a smile, she sang again. He could not keep himself from feeling drowsy. After a time, her voice became very low, and she sang in a language unknown to him, perhaps the language of her home. The melody seemed foreign, yet familiar. Its cadences held the artless sound of the ever-changing brooks that glisten in the dappled light of the forest, yet in that pure tranquility soared a wildness, like a falcon owned by no one. His breathing slowed as he drifted on the sound, and he was no longer Lancelot of the Lake but only a presence aware of that untroubled music, that song, entrancing still, as it turned to silence.

❡ The Lady kept vigil through the night. Then she sent for Lionel and asked him to have Lancelot's sword conveyed to the convent where the queen was buried. Then they went

together to the splendid tomb Lancelot had made for Galehaut, and where he himself would lie, close to his friend. The
Lady of the Lake departed, and Lionel was left alone to do what
was needed.

When Lancelot was laid to rest, Excalibur lay at his side.
And a new inscription appeared on the stone:

HERE LIES GALEHAUT,
THE SON OF THE GIANTESS,
LORD OF THE DISTANT ISLES,
WHO DIED FOR THE LOVE
OF LANCELOT
AND WITH HIM LIES
LANCELOT OF THE LAKE,
THE MOST VALIANT
OF ALL THE KNIGHTS
TO HAVE SERVED IN
THE KINGDOM OF LOGRES.

ACKNOWLEDGMENTS

At one stage or another in our collaborative undertaking, several friends have had the kindness to listen, read, and comment. We have benefited considerably from their suggestions and are happy to express our gratitude.

We thank Nancy Vine Durling, who has been a presence in this project since before its beginning; Charlotte Minard and Ida Rigby, who read penultimate versions; Aline Hornaday, who shared with us her specialized knowledge of the history that underlies our story.

To Patricia Stirnemann we offer thanks for helping us learn what we could from the iconography of medieval sources.

We thank Theodore W. Thieme for an early overview of the narrative, and we are deeply grateful to Jeffrey S. Ankrom for his sustained and perceptive interest in every aspect of our endeavor, from computer use to character analysis.

To David R. Godine we are immeasurably indebted for his untiring support of the project and for the most careful, intelligent attention that any editor-publisher could bestow upon a manuscript.

A NOTE ON THE TYPE

Lancelot and the Lord of the Distant Isles has been set in Golden Cockerel, a type designed in 1929 by Eric Gill for Robert Gibbings at the Golden Cockerel Press and used most famously in the press's *Four Gospels of the Lord Jesus Christ,* a volume frequently counted among the most beautiful books from England. Like most of Gill's type designs, Golden Cockerel bears a closer kinship to inscriptional letter forms than to historical typographic models. And while the roman hews closely to Gill's most popular face, Perpetua, the present type is significantly darker, giving pages a dramatic presence. The italic, derived from several Gill faces, was developed by the International Typeface Corporation to accompany its digital version of the roman, for which Gill never created an italic. ❖ The initials for the chapter openings have been drawn by Carl W. Scarbrough. They are modeled on a set of calligraphic capitals drawn by Graily Hewitt, the noted English lettering artist, for the Ashendene Press.

Design and composition by Carl W. Scarbrough